GEORGE ALEXANDA

Birch
SHADOW OF THE CAT

Fifty years had passed since the wars between the North and the South of Modania which had resulted in the imprisonment of Lord Zelfen in a place called the Watch; fifty years of peace and tranquillity during which boys had grown to men and prospered. But it was not to last. Lord Zelfen had a plan.

GEORGE ALEXANDA

Birch
SHADOW OF THE CAT

MEREO
Cirencester

Also by George Alexanda

Birch – The Beginning

Coming soon
Birch – The Swords of Modania

Published by Mereo

Mereo is an imprint of Memoirs Publishing

1A The Market Place Cirencester Gloucestershire GL7 2PR
info@memoirsbooks.co.uk | www.memoirspublishing.com

BIRCH - Shadow of the Cat

ISBN: 978-1-86151-094-5

For Jili Hamilton, with the greatest of respect and admiration

For Sid Pickersgill, my friend, my Minister and my rock

PROLOGUE

Within the timeless and multi-coloured mists of a far distant place, a place where no mortal men had ventured, three figures stood in silence on a white dais. After a while, one of them spoke. It was a voice like music.

"He sleeps." Calia, Goddess of Earth and Stone, looked down upon the land and smiled.

"Then let it be so." Eqwin, God of Wind and Water, appeared to be satisfied with the way things had turned out and was prepared to allow any future events to run their natural course. "Let time pass upon this land until the hour of the final confrontation" he said.

"Is this wise, Eqwin?" Frezfir, God of Ice and Fire, was in doubt. "Should we allow the situation to get out of hand once more? We are aware that Zelfen will try to escape, and we know that there will be a reckoning between him and Birch. However, we are unaware what form it will take. What if Zelfen triumphs over Birch? What then?"

Eqwin rested a friendly hand on his shoulder. "Frezfir my friend, you know that we cannot interfere with the destinies of humankind. There must be a natural progression toward what is to come, even if it does involve Zelfen."

"Then let us summon Master Elio. He's wise beyond years and would guide and advise those who would listen."

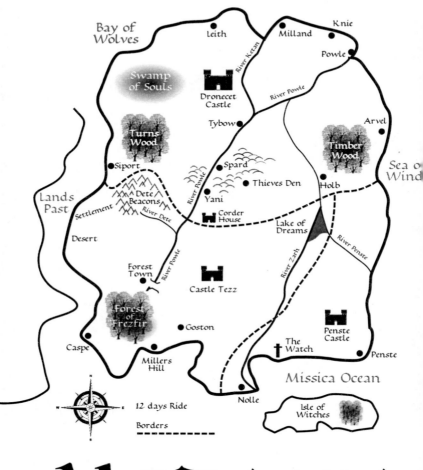

Bay of
Wolves

Leith

Knie

Milland

Powle

River Kezan

Swamp
of Souls

Dronecet
Castle

River Powle

Tybow

Arvel

Turns
Wood

Timber
Wood

Siport

Sea o
Wind

Spard

River Powle

Thieves Den

Holb

Lands
Past

Dete
Beacons

Yani

Settlement

River Dete

Corder
House

Lake of
Dreams

Desert

River Penste

River Powle

River Zath

Forest
Town

Castle Tezz

Goston

Penste
Castle

Forest
of
Frezfir

The
Watch

Penste

Caspe

Millers
Hill

Missica Ocean

Nolle

N

W   E

S

Isle of
Witches

12 days Ride

Borders

MODANIA

CHAPTER ONE

The clouds stretched to infinity like interwoven cotton-buds hovering on a background painted like thin pale blue ribbons. Drifting slowly, they traversed the sky on what appeared to be a never–ending journey. Fresh, invisible early evening breezes played games in endless scenarios. A lone eagle resting on the wind's currents sang its melancholy song, its immense wingspan supporting its streamlined body. It glided silently, smoothly. Its ebony eyes scanned the terrain along the curve of the earth for unsuspecting prey. Talons, its weapons of death, were ready to snatch the careless in their vice-like grip. Small, colourful birds chirped their love songs amidst the branches of the forest below. Pine needles and leaves added to the atmospheric effect as they fell to the ground in their own dramatic way, and laid a soft floor cushion on which small animals played. Constantly looking skywards, they were wary of the huge wingspan which hovered above them, the dark shadow which would signal instant death should they forego their vigil even for a moment, and allow the perfectly timed and co-ordinated actions of the eagle to give it its chance of an early evening meal.

Warmer breezes played games between the tall trees of the Forest of Frezfir, and carried the scents of a hundred different species along with them. The scents of aromatic flowers, the clean scent of pine, the scent of rotting wood festooned with fungi, forest scents, animal scents that gave a warning of friend or foe. Occasionally, hidden within the debris of the forest floor, small animals would lift their tiny heads above the leaves to sniff the air with little snuffling sounds for anything unusual that might prove to be threatening, or that might disturb their daily wanderings. Sometimes ill-timed curiosity gave opportunity to the black shadow above. Sometimes it resulted in the end of a small life to serve the needs of a larger one, the silent glider which, like a mail train, would take its consignment with precision and be gone in an instant.

In another part of the forest, equally silent, four huge paws belonging to an extremely large Timber Cat padded across the soft, pine-strewn blanket that was the forest floor. Constantly alert, two luminous green eyes that seemed almost too far apart scanned the area. Ears twitched, a wide black nose sniffed the air and sneezed, sending smaller animals scurrying to the safety of their homes underground. Birds chirped their alarm signals for a short time before settling back into their daily routines.

The immense black shape moved on as two more feet approached and followed it. These were human feet, silent feet which passed all areas of the forest as a kind of kindred spirit. Small animals acknowledged the familiar scents of the two unusual friends, and took little notice as they resumed their daily activities.

There was nothing to fear from these members of the community. They travelled the forest regularly to ensure that everything was as it should be.

Eventually the two travellers arrived at a small clearing. The huge black mass that was the Timber Cat stopped, stretched and yawned, displaying even rows of sharp white teeth. Then it sat down and began to clean itself with long, purposeful strokes of a deep pink tongue. The Timber Cat's immense frame occasionally shuddered and sent messages to over-attentive flies not to dwell too long on its smooth black coat.

A sound, and Cat turned its huge head to notice Birch as he stepped into the clearing. A smile crossed a youthful but knowledgeable face as he drew close to the cat. Birch seemed youthful in appearance, but his long black hair had begun to show signs of greyness creeping in at the sides above his rounded ears. How long had it been, he wondered as he sat by his companion? Images of the past floated across the mirrors of his mind. He remembered his learning with his adopted father, the woodcutter. He remembered the gift of the Timber Cat as a kitten and the happy times they enjoyed. He also remembered his uncontrollable emotion when the woodcutter had passed from his earthly life.

As Birch and the Timber Cat had grown together they had learned the secrets of magic under the tuition of Master Elio, and at the end of their tuition they had been gifted the mystical combination of singular travel, the gift of transformation by the gods. Cat would have the capability of merging with Birch where the huge feline might be thought of as a danger, and where the keenest of human senses were needed, especially in towns and other densely populated areas. On the other hand and where animal instincts served best, Birch could merge and travel within the Timber Cat. It was far better than entering a mind, it was being Cat or being Birch and yet being separate, with no side effects. The only way that anyone could detect this merging of the two bodies would be by examining the colour of the eyes, if they could get close enough. When Birch travelled within the Timber Cat, Cat's eyes would change colour from their usual green to an ice blue, and when the Timber Cat travelled within Birch, his eyes would change from blue to green.

Master Birch, Master over all Masters, could use magic continually, but magic and the use of it makes noise. The higher the degree of magic used, the louder the sound produced and the more people of the magical persuasion would notice. Ordinary people, those without the gifts of magic, could not sense or hear the rumble of magic waves, but to one who practised the arts it could be ear shattering. It could be likened to a migraine as it flashed across the temples of existence.

It had been so during the battle with Lord Zelfen many years ago, but Birch had always erred on the side of caution. Little did he know that Lord Zelfen had planned his escape, should Birch be victorious and Zelfen be trapped by the runes of the Watch. Time was the only obstacle; an obstacle that was about to be overcome. As the sun rested its great yellow orb on the horizon and the dark shadow of day's end began to creep over the land, all that could be heard was the constant buzz of insects and the occasional hoot of an owl.

"We will rest here for the night." Birch began bending young saplings, tying them at the tops to form a dome. Fallen leaves served as a covering to make a rough shelter from the night's chill breezes and clearing a small area he pointed his hand towards a small pile of sticks. A dazzling beam of light flashed from his fingertips and the sticks began to burn to create a warm glow. The Timber Cat immediately lay down in front of it and began to purr miniature drum rolls of contentment.

"You always do that" said Birch. The mock chastisement was ignored as Cat looked up, blinked, and then went back to her accustomed half-sleep. It was within the realms of possibility that the two companions could have continued their journey until they reached the timber-constructed cabin where, as a boy, Birch had been given a small black kitten which had grown to be his lifelong companion, but Birch occasionally liked the openness of the forest away from closed walls and memories.

As the sounds of the forest quietened and the dark shadows of night descended, the cracking of burning wood echoed through the trees and the firelight created its own drama as ghostly shadows played to an unseeing audience as Birch slept and dreamed. He dreamed of that night a time long ago. He dreamed of the friends he had made, Lords Torran, Brin, Karl and Edmund. In his dreams he remembered Lord Edmund's despair when Tamur, his friend and servant, had taken an arrow that was meant for him during the battle between North and South, and as a result had died shortly afterwards. He dreamed of the terrible onslaught of earth and stone that followed in the wake of Edmund's fury, his tears and his sorrow. He remembered how pleased and relieved he was when Edmund decided to give up his powers, for he could not control them when he was truly angered. He dreamed of the happiness that he and Lord Torran had shared when Lord Torran, the Wizard of Ice and Fire for so many centuries, decided to live a normal life and grow old and be remembered by his children. He dreamed of Lord Karl of Brin, Wizard of Wind and Water, who proudly held the banner of his household as he rode home from battle victorious. The three doves that at last truly meant peace after so much turmoil with so many casualties including the Lord Tezz, the first dove, the first peacemaker, who was overcome along with the Lady Tezz and friends by the enemy in the snow-deep forest. The sounds of steel meeting steel still echoed as ghostly mists played out their eternal production of the tragedy. They were disturbing dreams that weighed heavily on Birch's subconscious, not only because of their content, but because they were of a time long past. Why did he have these dreams now?

★ ★ ★

Lord Zelfen cursed as he paced to and fro. He kicked at the walls. He slammed his fist on the table that sat in the centre of the cell that was his prison. He vowed revenge upon those responsible for his internment.

"This land is mine!" he shouted to no-one. "It will be mine to do with as I please, and nobody shall stand in my way!"

His mind-set had not altered over the years; in fact his mood had darkened. The sounds of the sea, which he could clearly see from a small window, seemed to laugh at his isolation. Waves rumbled their delight at his rage. Sea foam danced by his window and spat in his black face.

"You will know my retribution in time," he shouted, but his pitiful endeavours to gather his will and bring his powers to bear were constantly thwarted. He was neutralised because his powers had been taken away by the strangely worked configurations that surrounded his prison and which he could not remove, the silver rune markings that covered all surfaces and which had been written there since the beginning of time. He had tried all things to escape; he had even tried to dig at the mortar that held the ancient stones of the building in place. His attempts to escape had resulted only in cracked and broken nails and bruised and bleeding fingers.

"I can still hear you, Birch. I know you are out there pandering to the wants and needs of the vermin that dwell in this land!" He roared. The words echoed, rebounded off the solid walls, but far from cooling his temper, imprisonment had only served to heighten it. From the start, days turned into weeks, weeks into months and months into years. His anger turned to loathing and his loathing into madness.

"How long must it be before someone finds the way to release me? It will happen, and when it does I shall have my revenge, Birch. I shall have my revenge!" The words again echoed throughout the building, were caught by the wind and carried away.

Unlike most members of the animal kingdom, who were able to sense present dangers, Cat appeared to have an added sense, the ability to see the possibility of future danger. She could not determine what that danger might be, or what form it would take, but she could tell if it was there lurking in the shadows of the future. Amid the half-sleep of Cat's dream-world the alarm bells of impending danger now began to ring and her luminous green eyes slowly opened and scanned the area. Just before daybreak she loped off into the dense forest in search of the source of those warning vibrations.

It was some time before Birch opened his eyes. He stretched and combed the hair from his face with his fingers as the sun played its warmth on the forest floor. Then, as he sat up, he noticed that Cat had departed. It didn't enter his mind to consider where Cat would be or even how long she would be away. He knew that his companion would return as she always did. He climbed from his night shelter and untied the saplings so that their release would assist in their growth. He said a mental thank you to them before covering the embers of the night's fire with earth so as to prevent accidental fire damage to the forest and its inhabitants. He then continued his journey, travelling along pathways only he knew, until, at last, he reached his destination.

The timber cabin stood before him, and he smiled. The broken window still needed replacing and the resting place of his adopted father needed tending. Birch was often away for long periods of time as he travelled throughout the land. Sometimes his journeys were short, but he always had a good feeling when he returned home to his own secret place within the Timber Wood.

Tybow was a comparatively new village constructed mainly of thatched cottages and was situated in the north of Modania a good two days' ride from Dronecet Castle. The village consisted of two rows of cottages through which one of the main roads to the castle ran. The main village industry was the construction of rope made from hemp, which was grown in nearby fields. One or two farmers bred and supplied cattle for the table and others grew cereal crops and vegetables, not only for the village but for the castle, and the community enjoyed steady but promising growth. As time passed the village became a haven for travellers, as it was the last stop for food and water for people travelling to Dronecet Castle and the North. The blacksmith's forge, a village necessity, was continually busy and good business was always concluded with the exchange of much-needed coinage. It had taken almost twenty years for the village to become self-sufficient and it had been a hard task for the founders. Now the occupants could look forward to a good and secure future.

The blacksmith was a founder member of the village, and he was overjoyed when his wife presented him with a son two years later. However, the son, whom the blacksmith had named Aluen, even as a child, seemed out of place as a smith's son. In contrast to his father, a well built and well-muscled man suited to his occupation, Aluen was small and thin for his age. He was almost weedy in his appearance. His cropped hair made him look more like a page boy than the son of a blacksmith. His appearance, however, was deceptive, for he was a strong youth, belying his looks. He regularly helped his father with his work at the forge, although his real ambition was to become a magician, and over a period of time he had accumulated a varied collection of items for the sole purpose of creating illusionary effects.

However, this did not satisfy him. He was convinced that real magic was possible and that it existed somewhere in the minds of men. He had heard stories from the old folk and from passing tradesmen that real magic existed, and he wanted to find it. He wanted to be able to use this elusive quality. He wanted it today. He wanted to become a real magician. At times during the summer season, weather permitting, Aluen would travel to summer fairs to meet with like-minded people who would be willing to share secrets that would both amaze and baffle his village audience. He was constantly on the lookout for something new, and his demonstrations delighted his friends, who were grateful for the occasional diversion from everyday life. As a result of his endeavours he was rewarded with produce from farms and fields.

A blacksmith grows nothing, so in lean times these gifts were well received by Aluen's parents and they gave him every encouragement to perform bigger and better illusions. Occasionally friends from the coastal regions came to visit with their twin daughters. On one occasion Aluen utterly confounded the audience with illusions that convinced them that a girl had disappeared, only for her to reappear at the back of the hall. Another time the audience was so engrossed with one of Aluen's illusions that they believed them to be real, and when Aluen appeared to be sawing a girl into two separate halves, one member shouted 'murder!' Calm had to be restored, but when the illusion was over the girl stood up completely unharmed. The audience shouted approval as she stepped down from the box.

Aluen's crowning moment was when he appeared to make two identical girls out of one. The villagers spoke about the performance for many weeks afterwards. Yet although successful as an illusionist, Aluen still wasn't satisfied. He wanted to perform real magic and not what he termed party tricks.

★ ★ ★

It was a quiet, hazy late spring morning when the messenger arrived. Flowers bloomed their reds, yellows and blues. Birds called their mates to nest and lambs frolicked in the fields. The villagers gathered at the meeting place in the centre of the village in order to hear the latest news and proclamations and Aluen, together with his parents, mingled with the crowds that had gathered. It was not only a time when news was given and received but an opportunity for businessmen to conduct negotiations for the coming season, it was almost like a market.

Among the many items of interest and the numerous business transactions, Aluen heard of the staging of a mystic fair. This was to be held at Dronecet Castle in mid to late summer and Aluen, hardly able to contain himself, decided that this was an event he did not want to miss. He began dancing in his excitement, much to the amusement of his parents and the villagers, who, caught up in the mood of the day, also began to dance along with him until soon the whole village was enjoying the festivities.

One of the messengers, for there were many, informed Aluen that the proposed mystic fair was attracting a great deal of interest and some interested parties were already arriving at the venue. It promised to be a huge event.

A black shadow observed the proceedings from a distance before disappearing once again.

★ ★ ★

Later, back at the smithy, Aluen was lost in his thoughts as he calculated what he would need for his forthcoming journey to the mystic fair. Already he had formulated a list in his mind, and with the help of his father he constructed a small but adequate horse-drawn cart. It was large enough to carry most if not all of the items that he wanted to sell or exchange.

His mother had busied herself in her kitchen baking cakes and bread for the journey. She told Aluen that even at mystic fairs people had to eat, and it would add another attraction to his stall.

Everything was going to plan, and soon the day of his departure arrived. Aluen awoke and rubbed the sleep from his eyes, washed in the cold spring water and then dressed himself for the journey. He peered out from his bedroom window to witness the beginning of another summer's day and noticed a black shadow in the distance. He blinked and looked again. The shadow was no longer there.

The morning dew slowly evaporated as the sun spread its warmth across the land and the birds welcomed the day with their songs. Aluen's mother, who had risen long before the others, as was her custom, had prepared a breakfast of honey and oats; not that Aluen was particularly hungry, because he was too excited. He was keen to be off on his journey, and with the help of both his parents he packed the small cart with the selection of items he had chosen to take with him. "Time for me to go," he told his parents as he climbed onto the cart, and with a wave of his hand he spurred the horse into action. His excitement and enthusiasm beamed on his smiling face as the horse pulled the cart away from his home. Along the way, other villagers waved to him as he passed crossing the village boundary and heading north. He set a brisk pace, and soon joined the main road that would take him to Dronecet Castle.

It was not long before he was joined by a stream of traders heading in the same direction. Some were travelling to buy goods for resale, others were performers like Aluen, who hoped to advance their knowledge in the arts. Along the road there were caravans with strange signs and lettering, heavily-laden carts, carriages and people walking. Aluen marvelled at the variety, and also at the clothes that people were wearing; mystical dress, some would have it. There were capes, oddly-shaped hats that made Aluen laugh, multi-coloured leggings. There were coats and full-length robes that added ceremony to the procession, and everyone seemed to be in a joyous mood. The midday sun shone its warmth on the procession, which added to the general well-being of the travellers.

Quite unexpectedly, as Aluen was not acquainted with anyone there, he was invited to share a meal with a mysterious-looking stranger. This traveller was of medium build, rounded in the middle and wore black robes with the strangest of silver rune markings on them, including a snake which was curled around a staff. His face seemed to be as old as time itself and yet there was a youthfulness about it which invited friendship. His long white beard reached almost to his waistline and his pale blue eyes were pools of knowledge.

"I hope that you take no offence," said Aluen, "but what does that insignia mean?" He pointed to the silver snake.

"Oh that," answered the man, tapping the design with a stubby finger. "Don't tell anyone, but I think it means I am a master magician." The man winked and tapped his nose with a finger. Aluen could not help but laugh at this amusing person. He began to admire him as they walked towards the man's caravan, and he was even more surprised when this unusual stranger produced a tray carrying a freshly-cooked chicken, fruit, nuts and a bottle of fine wine.

Aluen's eyes widened. "How on earth did you manage to prepare that?" he asked. He was still thinking of the possible ways of preparing the food when he was invited to sit and eat his fill.

"Oh, I had a little help" said the stranger after a little thought. Aluen thought it best not to press for an explanation in case the stranger was offended, but he continued to ponder the possibilities. This man was alone, yet he didn't have a fire burning on which to prepare the meal. No pots or pans could be seen, or cooking knives for preparation, and Aluen was a very observant young man. He made a mental note to watch for another such invitation in the future.

"Eat up Aluen, or you'll never be strong." The jovial character pointed to the food with a chicken leg. "I suppose you are wondering how I came to know your name."

"Well, it had crossed my mind."

"I had a little help," said the man again. Aluen laughed, and thought that he must have mentioned it during an earlier conversation.

"Well, as you know my name, do you think it would be possible for me to know what to call you?" asked Aluen, as politely as he could.

"Ummm… I suppose you can call me anything you like as long as you don't call me late for breakfast." Aluen giggled. He liked this stranger. He was amusing.

"No really, what is your name? I must call you something." Aluen began to pour two goblets of wine and took a mouthful.

"Some people call me Elio. Master Elio. Of course I am known by other names, but only when I am not listening," he smiled.

"Then with your permission I shall call you Master Elio."

"Of course you have my permission, now eat," he said with a wave of his hand towards the meal.

Little did Aluen know that this blue-eyed stranger who called himself Master Elio was indeed a master, of the art of magic, real magic, and that there was none to equal him in anything.

When they had eaten their fill, Master Elio stood up, shook the crumbs from his robes and stretched his legs.

"Shall I clean up and wash the plates, Master Elio? I feel obliged to help out, especially after you have supplied such a splendid meal."

"No, you need not do that, besides they will find their own way back," he replied, smiling.

Aluen didn't quite understand that last remark, but he decided not to ask for an explanation, it might have appeared to be disrespectful under the circumstances.

The two companions made ready to continue their journey, climbing onto their respective carts. Aluen looked back as the journey got under way only to notice that another strange event had taken place. The tray and plates that had contained the remains of the meal he had enjoyed, the wine, the goblets and hand towels, were nowhere to be seen. He was quite certain that Master Elio hadn't picked them up. It was extremely confusing. It was a fact that Aluen had been searching for real magic for so long that when he witnessed it first-hand, his mind either didn't register it, or would not accept that it was real magic. He had no idea that he was indeed in the company not only of a celebrated magician, but a bit of a rogue.

Master Elio had a lifetime habit of 'borrowing' things. It was something which he enjoyed and which, providing no harm came to anyone, gave him a certain amount of pleasure. It was believed in some circles that fifty years previously he, along with his horse, had disappeared during a conversation with some locals, scaring the living daylights out of them. Very few people remembered him now, and that was the way he liked things. Even Birch, his student at that time, had been forgotten except in the stories of myth and legend.

As Aluen and Master Elio journeyed on towards the fair at Dronecet Castle and the evening began to close in, many of the other travellers were beginning to make camp for the night. The daylight was fading and the night was beginning to creep over the green fields, hiding their colours. Seeing that Aluen was weary, Master Elio called a halt to make camp and after tending to their horses, the two companions sat in conversation around a small but adequate fire. The dark walls and the lights of Dronecet Castle could be seen faintly in the distance and still, even after all this time, it held some dark memories for Master Elio. It showed on his troubled face; his expression was like a black thundercloud. Even his horse, Ajax, was unsettled with distant memories.

"Is there anything wrong?" Aluen was concerned.

"Oh! Just thinking," replied Master Elio, having quite forgotten for a moment that Aluen was there. "Hungry?" he asked.

Aluen had been observing his companion. At no time had he had an opportunity to prepare anything, nor did he have anyone to help him.

"Just a little," he replied.

"Then perhaps we should try one of those cakes that your mother made for the journey." Master Elio giggled under his breath, knowing that Aluen was of an inquisitive nature and was still wondering where the earlier meal had come from.

"How did you know about the cakes? Oh don't answer that. You had a little help?"

"Something like that." He chuckled to himself, knowing that Aluen's little plan of discovery had come to nothing.

Aluen decided that Master Elio must have known his parents. Why else would this confusing person offer him friendship in the first place? He was probably there at the request of his parents to keep an eye on him and make sure that he didn't get into trouble.

The darkness of night had now fully descended. Stars twinkled in the velvety silence and a round moon smiled down from the heavens. Master Elio and Aluen sat staring into the flickering flames of the camp fire as sparks occasionally leapt into the night sky like miniature fireflies rising from the ground, the flames painting fiery shadows on their faces as Aluen began to drop off to sleep.

"Come along young man, it's time for you to retire. Go and get some rest, because it will be a big day tomorrow." Master Elio stood up and stretched some of the sleep from his bones. Aluen readily agreed, wandered off to his cart and returned with a blanket which he arranged next to the welcoming heat of the camp fire.

"Goodnight Master Elio," he said as he lay down and pulled the blanket tight around himself. After a while Master Elio returned the compliment, but by then Aluen was fast asleep. Elio smiled as he walked over to his wagon and bedded down for the night.

As the flames of the camp fire died down to leave a ragged circle of glowing embers surrounded by a halo of white ash, a huge dark shape slunk past his wagon. Two luminous eyes, two bright green slits of determination that seemed to be too far apart, looked over to the sleeping form of Aluen, saw that all was well and then disappeared into the night.

★ ★ ★

The morning came almost too quickly for Aluen; he was still feeling tired and blamed his condition on too much fresh country air. He stretched himself into consciousness. Master Elio had already put more logs on the fire and arranged breakfast, and the smell of cooked meats and eggs began to fill the air. Aluen was drawn to the rich aroma.

"Don't tell me Master Elio, you had a little help."

"Just a little," he admitted trying to hide his amusement. "Why don't you join me? There's plenty to go round."

"There's enough to feed another dozen besides." Aluen was certain that there was something strange about this old gentleman, but he was undecided as to what it was. He was also frustrated that he hadn't woken earlier. Had he done so he might have witnessed how Master Elio had prepared the food.

They sat in silence as they ate their fill and then prepared to continue their journey. This time Aluen didn't ask about cleaning up the breakfast dishes, he just looked at Master Elio, who in turn shrugged his shoulders and smiled.

"I know, they will find their own way back," suggested Aluen.

"Yes, they probably will."

Aluen was trying to pluck up courage to make further enquiries regarding the strange events that surrounded his companion, but he decided against it. He concluded that it was all illusion, and so the question in his mind faded away. The next day was uneventful with the exception of the mysterious meals, the preparation of which still eluded Aluen, but by the middle of the morning of the next day all seemed to be forgotten as the full extent of the mystic fair could be seen. Master Elio simply smiled, but Aluen was highly impressed, captivated by the massive range of it; it was immense. The stalls were many and varied and displayed all kinds of mystic paraphernalia. There were stalls with maps for sale purporting to show where hidden treasure could be found. There were stalls selling herbs and spices from distant lands, tunics, robes and remedies for almost every complaint from hair loss to ingrowing toenails. There were stalls selling books, fortune tellers, fire eaters, jugglers and carpenters who, for an arranged fee would offer their services and skills in the making of trap doors and magic boxes for the many illusionists who attended. A notice with the words 'Total confidence' was pinned to a carpenter's wagon.

There were snake charmers from distant places and even people who walked on fire and on needle-sharp beds of nails.

The ageing Lord Edmund, the one-time lord of Dronecet Castle, had retired to private life, leaving his son, Lord Tamur, who bore the name of a long departed but not forgotten friend, in charge. It was he who was the organizer and architect of the mystic fair. He hoped that he had covered every eventuality, every possibility, and as the lord of Dronecet Castle he awaited reports that all was going to plan.

He viewed the scene around the castle. There were hundreds of tents of varying colours and sizes, and all would pay a tribute depending upon their ability to do so. Lord Tamur smiled in satisfaction as the aroma of many different styles of cooking permeated the air with the offer of satisfaction or curiosity.

The road leading to the fair also formed an enormous circle which surrounded the castle. Soldiers from Lord Tamur's regiments directed the incoming visitors, asking each in turn to travel to the left so as not to cause confusion and delay and to make it easy for those leaving to navigate the exit. Of course as, with all large events, not all had come to spend or to make money honestly. Large crowds have always been and will always be a magnet to thieves, pickpockets and a whole host of tricksters. The castle guards were aware of this and were permanently on duty patrolling the event day and night to keep a watchful eye on the proceedings. This was not an easy task with so few trying to look after the interests of so many. A pickpocket could carry out his dreadful trade and then merge with the crowds and be lost from sight in a moment.

There are always exceptions, and the exception on this particular day was a supposed expert who, in his naivety, tried to steal Master Elio's purse as Elio walked the horse pulling his wagon through the entrance gate to the fair. When the would-be thief retracted his arm from Master Elio's person, his hand appeared to be missing. All that was left was the stump where the hand should have been. The pickpocket began screaming in terror to the people around, who failed to understand what he was raving about because to them his hand was still in plain sight. It was only the thief who could not see it. All he saw was a bloodied stump where his hand should have been.

The next moment the confused thief again screamed his fear and frustration when, instead of standing at the opening gate to the fair, he found himself up to his neck in the castle cesspit at the back of the fair. It simply wasn't his day.

"I wonder what all the commotion is?" enquired Aluen on hearing the screaming.

"Perhaps someone has thrown his hand in after having a bad day" said Master Elio. He smiled and urged Aluen onwards.

As Master Elio and Aluen led their respective vehicles into the fair proper, Aluen looked around for somewhere where he could set up his stall. He was rewarded at the first bend in the road, where an adequate space was available. He immediately began to unload and display his unwanted items, along with the remaining bread and cakes that his mother had baked. Master Elio wished him good fortune and thanked him for his company during the journey.

"Perhaps we will meet again?" Aluen called hopefully.

"Perhaps, my young friend, perhaps," and with that parting comment Master Elio disappeared into the tide of excited visitors.

Throughout the day Aluen beamed, as he was continually busy explaining to other illusionists in private the workings of hidden levers and partitions, showing the various pieces of equipment and arranging prices for prospective buyers. The cakes and the bread his mother had baked had long since been sold to hungry passers-by and Aluen's purse, large as it was, appeared to be bulging with coins. By late afternoon all of Aluen's surplus equipment had been sold at good prices and he was content with the outcome. He took the much-needed spare time to attend to his horse before looking around the huge fair for something that might attract his interest.

As the day drew to its inevitable close, a chill wind threatened a cold night. Camp fires began to appear as traders and customers alike began to settle down for the evening. The day's business had ended for most people, but the food vendors had huge pots filled with soups and stews which boiled their enticing aromas into the night sky. Aluen, who had managed to sell every one of his items on the first day, sat by his campfire enjoying a bowl of steaming hot stew. He was overjoyed with the amount of money he had made and was looking forward to the next day, when, with a list in mind, he would seek out some new illusions which, he hoped, would amaze the villagers back home. He also hoped that maybe he would find a book or two about the possibilities of real magic.

As he sat looking at the velvet sky with its millions of tiny stars reflecting the moonlight, he wondered how long it would take to travel to one. At least a few months of hard riding, he thought.

"Had a good day?" A patrolling soldier raised his hand in greeting as he passed.

"An extremely good one, thank you," Aluen waved back with a smile.

"Good night then, sir." The soldier saluted before continuing a conversation with his fellow patrolmen.

A dark shadow moved slowly and secretively through the camp.

"Goodnight." Aluen was feeling a little important. "Sir" he thought. It made him feel good and to add to this, as a small non-professional stall holder, he had very little to pay for permission to sell at the fair. He was asked only for a small donation to cover his registration. It was only professional market traders who were asked to pay a tithe to the lord of the castle. The money collected was not entirely for profit. It was used to pay cleaners, land workers and soldiers for their extra duties. The lord of the castle had also incorporated a goods protection scheme, a kind of insurance. Soldiers were invariably sent to seek out anyone with ill intent in a bid to save the stallholders' property or takings, but sometimes the thief would escape. Any person who had proof of theft where the offender had evaded capture was fully compensated for their loss by the castle treasury. This was very popular with traders and even regular markets were well attended.

Aluen walked round the outskirts of the multi-coloured tents. For some reason it seemed that he was walking on a cushion of air, his feet not touching the ground. It was a strange feeling because it appeared that he was being guided. Then the sensation disappeared as quickly as it had started.

In front of him a few feet away Aluen noticed a scroll lying on the ground. It was protruding above a thin mist that swirled in the light breeze. He bent down to pick the scroll up, but as he did so he heard a low growling noise to his right. He looked up to see two green luminous eyes staring at him from a distance through the mist. The wind suddenly became stronger and the scroll was blown further away from him. He ran forward, but as he again bent down to pick up the scroll, a black mass leapt upon his back. Aluen suddenly sat upright, sweat dripped profusely from his forehead, and then realised that he had been dreaming. As he settled down again in his half-awake state he saw a large black Timber Cat slowly walk past him and disappear into the shadows.

No, it couldn't have been, he thought. There was no cry of alarm. The horses were not in distress. No one seemed to have noticed. Eventually he managed to sleep but while he slept, the two luminous green eyes watched from a distance. An elderly-looking man wearing a black robe with silver markings on it gently ran his fingers through Cat's thick black fur and Cat, contented, purred her miniature drum rolls of satisfaction, for she had known Master Elio for many years.

The morning sun slowly dried the moist earth and Aluen's sleep was invaded by a steady increase in the volume of noise coming from the activity at the fair. Another day of trading had begun. He sat up and scratched his head as he recalled the dream of the previous night; it disturbed him. He yawned before rolling up his blankets and dropping them unceremoniously into his empty cart. Before he decided to investigate what was on offer for sale at the fair, he attended to the needs of his horse, patted its rump and spoke to it softly.

"It will not be long now before we can head for home" he murmured. The horse seemed to understand and nodded its head, stamping its hooves in anticipation.

Aluen set off, keeping his hand on his purse as a precaution, and began to browse over the many stalls still remaining. After a while he stopped at a stall where many different types of box were displayed; they included one he recognised, having sold it himself on the previous day. The trader, who remembered Aluen, came forward and greeted him with a warm handshake before inviting him to see something special.

"It's a death box," the trader explained. "I will show you how it works." He called one of the young girls who worked for him, and asked her if she would be his assistant during a demonstration. The girl readily agreed. The trader placed the girl inside a narrow upright box and locked her in. Then, showing Aluen several razor-sharp swords, he proceeded to insert them one by one at angles through the box. Aluen could clearly see the girl's face through a small, specially-designed opening at the top of the box. Suddenly, as the final sword was pushed through the box, the girl screamed and her head dropped. A red liquid seeped from the bottom of the box and Aluen feared that the young girl had been killed. Then, with a flourish, the trader removed the swords, letting them fall to the ground for effect, and opened the box. Smiling, the girl walked out completely unharmed.

Aluen was amazed, and urged the trader to tell him how the mechanism worked. For the next hour the trader explained in detail how to accomplish several different effects using red ink and a variety of attachments. The meeting was in private to keep the workings of the box a secret. After some rather extensive bargaining, Aluen and the trader agreed on a price, providing help would be given to move the heavy box to his cart.

When Aluen had secured the box with covering sheets and rope, he wandered back to the fair to continue his search for other things of interest. He found the selection of all things supposedly magical fascinating. Eventually he purchased several books from one stall and from another some powder that, when ignited with a burning stick, produced coloured smoke clouds, which could add effect and mystery to his demonstrations.

He was about to return to his cart when he saw in a field, just beyond the line of tents, what appeared to be a scroll of parchment blowing idly in the slight breeze. He remembered his dream and nervously looked around to see if there was a black timber cat in the area. After a few moments, and seeing that there was no immediate danger, his curiosity had to be satisfied. He walked over to the scroll and bent down to pick it up but kept an eye open for any danger. The images of the dream still haunted him, but nothing happened and he was relieved that the full dream was not re-enacted.

He made his way back to his cart, sat down and unrolled the scroll of parchment to see what was written on it. In large letters which were decorated by markings that Aluen had never seen before, he read the following:

SEA DON'T GIVE ME AWAY
IN BUILDINGS ROUND, AND MIND
THE LETTERS TAKEN ONE BY ONE
A FORTUNE THERE TO FIND

Aluen almost threw the scroll away because it reminded him so much of his dream. Too convenient, he decided. However, he reconsidered the matter; it was an old scroll and it did present a challenge, if only to solve a riddle. He pushed the scroll into his belt before preparing his horse and cart for the journey home.

As he slowly pulled away from the fair, from a distance, he was being watched by a huge black shadow. An elderly-looking gentleman who wore long black robes covered with silver markings nodded his approval.

However, they were not the only ones who were watching Aluen's departure from the fair. There were four more pairs of eyes watching, greedy eyes eager to relieve Aluen of his hard-earned money.

It was late when Aluen started his homeward journey, but this was deliberate, for he wanted to arrive home by the evening of the following day. He didn't want to get there too early because he would have been expected to give an account of his travels and he would be tired. By arriving late in the evening any talk of adventure would have to wait until the following day, by which time Aluen would have had the benefit of a night's sleep.

As the darkness of night began to close in Aluen, feeling secure, made a camp fire. He sat alone missing the company of Master Elio and especially his meals, although he still didn't understand how he had managed to prepare them.

Unknown to him, four would-be robbers were now silently heading in the direction of his campsite. Unfortunately for them, as they came near they were met by two large luminous green eyes, two very unfriendly luminous green eyes, and an old man who was wearing a black cloak with silver markings. Immediately they turned and fled. How they managed to end up in the cesspit at Dronecet Castle they never knew. It was most unpleasant.

Aluen knew none of this. "Who's there?" he said, leaping to his feet.

"Only me," replied Master Elio. "I saw your encampment and thought I might keep you company for a spell." He giggled inwardly at his small play on words as he neared Aluen's camp fire.

"Hello again, Master Elio" replied Aluen. I would be honoured if you would keep me company. I'm afraid that I have very little left in the way of food, but you are welcome to share what I have."

"Oh, I have a few odds and ends of food about my person," replied Master Elio as he fumbled through his robes and produced some sliced meats, bread, nuts and a bottle of the finest wine. Aluen almost fell backwards with laughter. This was an amazing person, he thought. He considered introducing him to his parents upon his return to his village.

"I had a little help," explained Master Elio before Aluen could ask any questions. "Perhaps I can ride with you for part of your journey. My wagon appears to have developed a fault. I have left it at the castle so that repairs can be made."

"It will be my pleasure, and I will be glad of the company. By the way, I found this scroll at the fair. It was a strange experience because I dreamed about finding it the night before." He took out the scroll and handed it to Master Elio.

"Mmm. It's a riddle," said Master Elio.

"Yes, I have been trying to work out what it means."

"Well I don't think I can help you this time. I'm not very good at solving riddles. To me the only thing that appears to stand out as being strange is the word "sea". It is spelled S-E-A as opposed to S-E-E. There are two different spellings with two different meanings and the word used here appears to be in the wrong context. Or is it?"

Master Elio of course knew exactly what the scroll meant, but he could not tell Aluen. He wasn't allowed to interfere too much with the destinies of man.

Aluen slept a deep and untroubled sleep that night, totally unaware that a huge black shadow was keeping a constant watch. As the day's sun peeped over the horizon and sent its warm rays rolling over the landscape, birds began to chirp their morning songs. Master Elio and Aluen had risen early and made a camp fire, and Elio had begun cooking a breakfast of pancakes and honey. He had set a container of water to boil, then, producing a lemon from somewhere beneath the folds of his robes, he sliced it up and dropped the slices into the boiling water along with a little honey.

Aluen scratched his head as he observed the proceedings.

"What are you making with that yellow thing?"

"Lemon water," replied Master Elio. "It's a little sour to the taste, but quite refreshing and it will keep away the chills."

"You are making lemon water?"

"Yes, lemon water."

"It's quite... er... different." Aluen sat down as he sipped the hot drink.

"It's an acquired taste," Master Elio smiled to himself.

"Nice, though."

"Yes it is," replied Master Elio.

"I've never seen a... er... lemon before. Where did you...?"

"I had a little help," said Master Elio, cutting off the rest of Aluen's enquiry.

They ate breakfast in silence except for the sounds of birds singing their morning tunes and the whisper of the wind through the trees. Master Elio stretched his arms, masking a deliberate movement of his fingers, and two large fish suddenly appeared in front of the Timber Cat some distance away. She ate her breakfast in silence too. She cleaned her paws with long deliberate strokes of her tongue before moving forward. She sensed that Master Elio and Aluen had finished their breakfast and were making ready to continue their journey.

She inspected their night's encampment before disappearing into the shadows. It was as the sun rested above the distant tree tops on the third night that the lights of Aluen's village could be seen in the distance. Master Elio made his apologies to Aluen, saying that he had a long way to go and there would be little time to accept his invitation to visit his parents.

"Maybe another time," he said apologetically as he waved his goodbyes.

"I hope so," called Aluen. He was a little disappointed as he turned his horse and headed for home.

★ ★ ★

In the void above the land, in the timeless clouds of man's infinite imagination, in man's dreams and prayers where no earthborn being had ever set foot, three ageless figures stood motionless on a white dais. That which was spoken was the law.

"And so the seed is set. Let us watch it grow," said one of the figures.

"Yes we can watch, but we must not interfere," said another. "The destiny of man must be guided by his own hand, whether it is for good or whether it is for bad. For this reason I have cleansed the Swamp of Souls. The spirits that lay within will no longer impede man's progress."

The third figure remained silent for a while before asking a question. "What of Master Elio and Birch? They still have powers far beyond that of any normal man. Will they remain on earth? I believe that we have interfered for far too long and we should allow natural things to take their course."

"Do you suggest that it was wrong to appoint the three wizards in the first place?" asked the second figure.

"This may be the case or it may not, but on reflection I believe it was unwise. The use of magic for the control of the elements did speed creation, but the cost in terms of life was too much. We have lost our brother Zelfen because of our actions."

"We did not," interrupted the third figure. "Zelfen was not of our plan. He was and is a selfish lord. Whatever we did was for the betterment of the earth. He would see it in ruins for his own enjoyment. There can be no ruler of the earth with that kind of power, because it would lead only to corruption and misery. Evil would reign and man would be subdued to live a life of terror. No, there must be a system of government whereby all are equal, and it must be created by man alone. That cannot be achieved until this power and the ability and the will to use it have been removed from the earth. So it has been said on the dais, so it shall be.

"There remains only one question, and this concerns Lord Zelfen. We have agreed that all power and the ability to create magic should be removed from the earth. What if Lord Zelfen wins the forthcoming contest? Of course it is my hope that all will be well and our plans will succeed."

"But what if our plans do not succeed and Zelfen does win the contest? Shall we intervene then?"

"We have pledged that we shall no longer interfere with the ways of man. If Lord Zelfen wins the forthcoming contest, all will be lost."

The three figures stepped down from the dais and went their separate ways.

CHAPTER TWO

It was darker now, and grey smoke lazily climbing from a dozen chimney stacks seemed to peer through the evening mist. The scene gave the village an almost eerie feel as Aluen neared the outskirts. The blacksmith's workshop was not unlike a centrepiece for the village and was the last to close for the evening, its forge now only glowing embers as the day's work had been concluded. Aluen steered his horse and cart to a halt outside. His parents came out to greet him as was the custom, thankful for his safe return. Holding a lantern aloft, his mother called to him.

"Is that you, Aluen?"

"Who else would be out riding at this time of night, Mother?" He climbed down from the cart and embraced his parents. He was eager to tell them of his journey, the fair and the scroll he had found. He handed a bulging purse to his father with a smile. It was the custom that the head of the family would deal with all financial matters and keep safe the family finances.

"You have done well by the feel of the purse, Aluen."

"Yes Father I did and I had a wonderful time. Mother's cakes and bread were well received too."

His mother blushed as they all went into the cottage. A large iron pot which contained a stew had been simmering over an open fire and as a bowl of the steaming food was prepared for him, Aluen told his story of the fair. He described the castle and the colours of the tents, what was for sale and the size of the mystical fair, which dwarfed other fairs that he had attended.

"You should thank your lucky stars that you were not set upon by thieves," said his father who indicated the purse that now sat on the shelf above the fireplace.

"I had nothing to fear, Father. Soldiers from the castle regularly patrolled the area and no one would dare steal anything from under their watchful eyes."

Little did Aluen know just how close he had come to being robbed. If it had not been for the intervention of Master Elio and Cat, he would have been robbed, or worse. He went on to describe in detail the multi-coloured tents, the fair, the various items for sale including the things which he had purchased, the sometimes bizarre assortments of food and of course the atmosphere, which was unlike any other he had experienced.

"It was like no other fair," said Aluen excitedly. "Do you know Father, a soldier called me 'sir'? He actually called me 'sir'. Would you believe it? Then of course there was my travelling companion, Master Elio."

"Master Elio?" His father appeared confused.

"Yes Father. He was a really nice old gentleman who seemed to have a mysterious way of preparing food. I never did find out how he did it but I thoroughly enjoyed his company and I will miss him."

"Do you know, I am sure I have heard that name before" said his father. "However it could not have been the same person, because I was a child at the time. What do you mean when you say that he had a mysterious way with food?"

Aluen explained how Master Elio had offered him meals that could only have been prepared in a castle kitchen, and yet there were no facilities at hand to accomplish this.

"That's it!" Aluen's father appeared excited. "Wait a moment." He hurried out of the cottage to a neighbour's home, where he began to bang on the window. After a few minutes a sleepy face peered down from upstairs. Bony fingers scratched an unruly mop of grey hair.

"What is all the commotion and banging? Is there a fire in the village?" The occupant rubbed his tired eyes.

Aluen's father, a respected man in the community, asked the neighbour to join him. He said that he would explain, and expressed the urgency of the matter, saying that what he had to say could not wait until the morning. The matter must be discussed and could they speak together now?

The neighbour, an elderly man, lived alone, having retired from service some twenty years previously. In fact he was the oldest person in the village, according to some residents, and this was the reason why Aluen's father had woken him rather than anyone else.

The noise of a creaking staircase, a hat stand accidentally knocked over and the sound of cursing was followed by the door being opened. The neighbour was further startled when he was taken by the arm and escorted, still wearing his night clothes, to the blacksmith's cottage. When they arrived the neighbour was ushered into the kitchen and offered a seat at the table where, as was the custom, he was served a bowl of steaming rabbit stew which he accepted with a polite nod of his head.

"Now then," said the neighbour after he had eaten his fill of the tasty supper. "What appears to be the problem that caused you to drag me from my bed?

Surely it wasn't simply to ask my opinion on this wonderful meal. If it was, your good lady should be commended."

"No, but I would like you to listen to Aluen's story of his journey to and from Dronecet Castle. In particular I would value your opinion when you hear the description of his travelling companion."

Aluen stepped forward. "He was sort of old," began Aluen, "but not old if you know what I mean."

"Ageless," suggested the neighbour.

"Yes," continued Aluen. "He had a huge beard and he was wearing a black robe which was decorated with all sorts of strange silver markings sewn onto it."

The neighbour held up his hand to signify that Aluen should pause for a moment. "Did this black robe have any particular markings that you may be able to recall? For instance, did the robe have as one of its markings, a snake?"

"Why yes," replied Aluen. "It was a snake which appeared to be coiled around a staff. He was a chef or something, because he knew how to prepare food."

"Tell me about the food, Aluen." The neighbour was suddenly very interested in what Aluen had to say.

"Well, it was extremely tasty. It was as if it had been prepared for a lord of some castle and not something I would expect as a traveller."

"And did you witness the preparation of this extremely tasty food?"

"Actually I didn't. I was curious as to how the gentleman managed to prepare such food, but my curiosity was never satisfied."

"Hmm. Did this gentleman tell you his name?"

"Yes, it was….."

"Master Elio?" interrupted the neighbour.

"How did you know?" Aluen was surprised.

"Well I'll be blessed. He is still alive after all this time."

"Have I missed something here?"

"son," the neighbour said calmly. "Missed something? You are so naïve. You haven't the faintest idea who this person was, have you?"

"What have I missed?" Aluen sounded almost apologetic.

"I am sorry. I meant no offence," continued the neighbour. "Did this Master Elio have white hair?"

"Yes."

"Did he have a beard that grew down to his waist?"

"Yes."

"Was he of a jovial disposition, with a sort of cheeky smile?"

"Yes, but will you please come to the point."

"Aluen, I am stunned. I am lost for words. The person who you know as Master Elio is in fact the world's most powerful magician. He is older than

46

time and is probably related to the gods themselves and you, a mere boy, have had the pleasure and the privilege of his company. Do you know that people would have fought for the same privilege? You are indeed fortunate, young man, to have travelled with Master Elio. Did you know that he used to steal the food you shared? Many a time when I was in service, before and during the great wars, whole trays piled with the finest foods would fade into nothingness and vanish. Wine, hams and cheeses of the best quality would simply disappear. We would tell the other workers not to worry because the empty silver trays would reappear on the following morning. I wonder who he has been borrowing from lately."

For a moment he was lost in a dream of yesteryear. Aluen and his parents could almost share the moment with him and imagine the images being created, conjured up in the old gentleman's mind; images of his youth and the things he witnessed.

Aluen was excited. "Do you mean to tell me that Master Elio could perform real magic and I had no idea?"

"son," continued the neighbour, "Master Elio could turn you into a clothes peg if he so desired, just by blinking or twitching his nose." He blinked his eyes and twitched his nose to add emphasis to the description. A startled Aluen jumped back, which made everyone laugh. He thought of going outside to try to catch up with Master Elio, but was advised that he could be anywhere in the universe by now.

"I was actually accompanied by the most powerful man in the world. I wonder why?" Aluen retired to his room leaving the question unanswered.

The neighbour, after wishing the blacksmith and his wife the remainder of a good evening, returned to his home, but the question stayed on everyone's lips. Why had Master Elio met up with and accompanied Aluen on his journey; was it by chance?

As the village lights dimmed one by one, a large black shadow passed the blacksmith's workshop and headed out to green fields and shelter.

★ ★ ★

The following day a chill wind blew from the North, a sign that the seasons were changing. Aluen, along with his parents and the gentleman from the cottage next door, stood in the blacksmith's workshop next to the welcoming heat of the forge. Aluen displayed his purchases from the mystic fair, then, as they all sat around a small table, they began to discuss the scroll that Aluen had found.

"As Master Elio pointed out to me," began Aluen pointing to the writing on the parchment, "the word 'sea' has been misspelled. It should read 'see' unless it was a deliberate mistake."

"I would say that it was indeed a deliberate mistake," remarked the neighbour. "Parchments are written by learned people, so mistakes are not commonplace. If this were the case and a mistake had been made then the parchment would have been destroyed and another one written. It's a matter of pride. You told us that Master Elio had pointed out the different spelling of the word. This makes me certain that it was in fact a deliberate mistake, maybe part of a riddle and one that should be noted. There is to my mind something very special about this parchment. I say this because if it were nothing but a mistake, Master Elio would have dismissed it out of hand with a few words about the capabilities of the writer, but he didn't and this makes me very curious. The only way to find out what the writing on the parchment means is to decipher it. Now let me see."

The small company laughed at the unintended joke.

"Sea don't give me away" he said, quoting from the scroll.

"Something in the sea?" prompted Aluen's father.

"Perhaps something near the sea?" suggested Aluen.

"Don't give me away," continued the neighbour.

"Perhaps you are meant to keep this a secret, or maybe it suggests that you should not throw the scroll away. The words 'and mind' could mean 'be careful'. I'm afraid that I can't understand the rest. There are eighty-two letters in the wording, which could mean a fortune in letters. A building round.... round where?"

"I'm going to find out," announced Aluen. "I shall travel on the coast road which is nearest to the sea and I will ask a few questions of the local people to see if I can unravel the meaning of the scroll. Do I have your permission to go, Father?"

"As long as you go about your task carefully my son, but beware of strangers."

"I shall take my magic boxes and other tricks. It might give me a source of income. It would pay my expenses rather than having to ask you for money, Father."

"You have raised a good boy there, blacksmith," said the neighbour. "Take good care Aluen and come back to your family safe and sound."

"And hopefully with a fortune," replied Aluen.

★ ★ ★

"He has to grow up some time, so it might as well be now," said his father when his mother expressed her worry about the intended journey. So it was that Aluen was allowed to go. Later, fully rested and clothed for colder weather, Aluen set off with his cart laden with mystical illusions and supplies to seek the answer that lay hidden within the writing on the parchment.

At the moment when Master Elio had used strong magic to transport the would-be thieves into the cesspit at Dronecet Castle, Birch had been resting, listening to the night sounds of the forest. A soft glow of light from a single oil lamp seemed to add to the overall effects of tranquillity, but the sound of magic disturbed his peace. It was the first time since the wars that he had heard the rumbling sound, and he had become unaccustomed to the magical vibrations. It was like a drum beating in his ears. So quick was the spell that Birch had difficulty in locating its source. He knew however that only a master of magic could have made so speedy a delivery followed by such a loud report. He sat for a while contemplating what action, if any, he should take. He concluded that this incident needed investigation.

As the morning dawned Birch looked up at a grey sky. Birds in v-shaped formation were flying to their winter feeding grounds. Leaves were turning yellow and falling gently to the ground. Only the firs and pine trees defied the weather in their winter green.

Birch clothed himself with a thick woollen tunic and woollen leggings before gathering provisions for what could turn out to be a long journey. He sent his thoughts out to Cat and finally located her in the North of the country almost six days' journey away.

For reasons Birch could not understand at the time, Cat did not respond to her companion's call. Unknown to Birch, Cat had been given instructions from a higher authority. She had been asked to watch over Aluen to make sure that he came to no harm. If Aluen failed in his mission to discover the meaning of the riddle on the parchment, then the final confrontation would not take place at the appointed time. Only Aluen, an innocent, could give himself to this task. Little did he know just how dangerous the task would be.

★ ★ ★

The walls of Castle Tezz had not altered; they still looked the same as they appeared to rise defiantly out of the morning light. The castle colours, white doves on a background of pale blue, were hoisted aloft as the night watch galloped across the drawbridge. The sounds of the horses' hooves echoed their departure. Birch fancied that he saw Captain Da'cra lead the troops, the captain's highly polished boots and immaculate uniform a ghostly beacon in the swirling mist. Birch smiled at the memory for Captain Da'cra had been dead for many years. It was shortly after the wars between North and South had ended that the Captain had left Castle Tezz on a fact-finding journey to the Border House via Forest Town. He had wanted to check crops, buildings and the morale of the local inhabitants but he met with a band of Northern renegades who were intent on continuing the war.

The fight was short, as the Captain was attacked on all sides. His life ebbed away as his horse, trained in the way of battle, returned to Castle Tezz. Soldiers openly wept and beat their chests in frustration when the news of the tragedy was relayed to them. Many were on horseback in seconds and the soldiers of Castle Tezz exacted a terrible revenge upon the renegades, for they had murdered a most beloved leader of men. Lord Brin himself had led the search for the renegades, and when their camp was finally located at the foot of the Dete Beacons after several days of intense searching, he gave no direct order.

"Do your duty to a fallen comrade," were his only words.

Suddenly the air was filled with the cries of soldiers consumed with blood lust. "For Da'cra", the men shouted. The battle-hardened troops gave no quarter as they charged the renegades.

Not wanting to interfere in his soldiers' personal grievances, Lord Brin watched from a distance as screams of mercy went unheeded. Sword, mace and lance did their terrible work as soldiers fixed on vengeance were consumed with a blood lust they could not control. Even when the renegades had been reduced to lifeless bodies the soldiers continued to stab, slice and gouge in an insatiable need to avenge their fallen commander. Many cried as the emotion finally subsided and they headed back to Castle Tezz. The now unrecognisable bodies of the slaughtered renegades were left for old wives to tell stories and for nature to deal with. Many a tale was told of that incident and many songs were sung about the Captain.

The memory faded as Birch stood upon the castle drawbridge, his feet wet with the morning dew. As the mist cleared, two smartly dressed, uniformed guards looked in puzzlement at the lone figure who stood at the castle entrance. There was an air of confidence about him, but his appearance suggested that he was not a man of means.

"Who seeks entrance to the Castle Tezz?" called one of the guards.

"Birch," the reply was short.

"Then enter, Birch, and state your business."

The guards had been trained to expect the unexpected and so, as Birch walked slowly into the castle grounds through the lattice-worked iron gates, the soldiers kept a wary eye on this stranger and two guards escorted him to the reception area of the gatehouse.

"Have you come to visit anyone in particular?" asked one of the guards as though in passing conversation.

"I have come to visit Torran of Ice…" Birch hesitated. "I have come to visit with Lord Torran," he corrected himself.

"My apologies" continued the guard "but the Lord Torran will still be in his bed chamber, as is most of the castle at this time in the morning. Maybe you would like to come back later or if you prefer, you could wait."

"I'll wait," replied Birch.

"Then I will send a messenger as soon as protocol allows." The soldier saluted, although he didn't know why, and then with a smart turn he returned to his duties at the gate.

Birch sat on a low stool in the gatehouse and looked around him. The stone-built room was basically of a military appearance. There were no soft furnishings to accommodate visitors and this gave it a cold feeling. The walls were decorated with a collection of mismatched swords, each bearing a label denoting who the owner was, or to whom it had once belonged.

Three torches on each wall left black tapering traces of soot which seemed to point to a beamed ceiling. Sitting centrally at the far end of the gatehouse was a large wooden military-style desk and to the right, a row of four unoccupied cells. Behind the desk an open log fire kept the room moderately warm.

"What's your business with Lord Torran?" asked a rather rotund soldier who stood in front of the fire. He immediately sensed that he was asking the wrong question. Birch's stare was cold and hard, not to mention somewhat worrying. "For the books," he said as an afterthought. "We keep a record of everyone who visits the castle and there is a space for you to make a comment on your visit," continued the nervous soldier by way of explanation.

He did not know what made him nervous, but there was something strange and unsettling about this visitor. Maybe it was the visitor's eyes and the way they appeared to drink in all that they surveyed. Maybe it was the fact that this visitor had simply disappeared. One minute he was standing in front of the desk, then he wasn't. The soldier ran to the alarm bell.

"You need not sound the alarm on my account," said Birch. "We don't want to waken the whole castle, do we?"

The trembling soldier turned around to see Birch sitting on the desk. "But... but... you weren't here a minute ago, you... you..."

"Just to demonstrate that I have no ill intent," interrupted Birch. "I was here. You just didn't notice me."

"Yes, that must be the case. I'm a little tired because I have been on duty all night." The soldier wiped his sweating forehead with the sleeve of his tunic.

Birch smiled. It was the kind of smile that anyone could easily have drowned in. The soldier relaxed and immediately felt at ease.

"I have some business with the Lord Torran," explained Birch. "Unfortunately it is of a very private nature you understand, but be assured that all is well. The Lord Torran and I have known one another for a very long time. We are friends."

"I'll just put down the visit as a business meeting then, shall I?" enquired the soldier.

"That will do fine." Sometimes you have to make a person nervous before they can relax, thought Birch.

★ ★ ★

"Do you have to start on me every morning, bowlegs?" Master Terance was getting dressed and trying to put on his leggings while hopping about on one leg.

"Philanderer!" shouted Master Errol.

"Mouse droppings!"

"Egghead!"

"Flatface!"

"You… you… you…"

"Excuse me Master Errol," interrupted a servant.

"Yes, Derik?" Master Errol tried not to smile.

"There is a person seeking an audience with Lord Torran, sire. He waits at the gatehouse."

"My father is still in his bed and should not be disturbed until he is ready to receive visitors."

"Should I ask the person to return at a more convenient time, sire?"

"Hmm. No, Derik. I shall attend to it."

"As you wish, sire."

The servant left the room as Master Errol finished dressing. "I shall be back shortly, pig's breath." Master Terance laughed and made a rude sign.

"Run out of words? My departure will give you time to think of some, snot face."

They were like brothers, Errol and Terance, and although Master Errol was two years the elder nothing could separate them. Their game of insults, a continuation from years gone by when their respective fathers used the same to annoy their enemies and have fun with each other had become commonplace, much to the annoyance of their teachers of etiquette. Master Errol was not only like his father in the way he acted, he was the image of him in his appearance. His straight blond hair was worn long and his eyes were identical to his father's, ice blue with a steely stare. In a certain light, the men could almost be mistaken for twins.

Wearing a simple white robe tied at the waist with a light blue sash and light blue woollen leggings, Master Errol shivered slightly as the cold air of the morning greeted him. He walked across the parade ground towards the gatehouse, wondering who the visitor could be, and why he had chosen to visit his father at this early hour. Two guardsmen stood to attention and saluted Master Errol as he passed them, relaxed only when he had entered the gatehouse. Birch was stunned by the appearance of this young stranger as he entered the room set aside for visitors. It was Lord Torran, but there again it couldn't be, not after all the years had passed.

"Please accept my apologies for keeping you waiting, sir. My name is Master Errol. My father, Lord Torran, has not yet awoken from his bed, but maybe I could be of assistance?"

Birch looked at the man more closely and circled around him, much to the annoyance of the guards who were preparing to arrest this stranger. The similarities between Master Errol and his father, Lord Torran, were remarkable.

"I am amazed, Master Errol. I am almost speechless," said Birch. "The likeness... you could almost have been Torran. I..."

"Sir" interrupted Master Errol. "My father has a title as well as a name. It would indeed be bad manners not to use it."

Even as Master Errol spoke, Birch heard a voice from the past. "I am grateful for the lesson in manners, Master Errol...the shock of the likeness to your father unsettled me, please understand."

"I am afraid that I don't understand, Master...?"

"Birch, Master Errol. My name is Birch."

"Good heavens... not *the* Birch?"

"I am that person, Master Errol."

Master Errol immediately began to look around. He checked the rooms and even looked behind the chairs on which they had been seated.

"I see that your father also told you about Cat."

"Yes he did. Is she here?"

"No, she is not with me today. She has ... other commitments."

"Well, Master Birch, please don't just stand there, give me your hand in friendship. I'm sure that under the circumstances my father would be most upset and very offended if I failed to wake him."

★ ★ ★

Wherever there are people in the world that are ruled by a government, there are people who want that government to do more than is possible. The more concessions that government makes, the more those people want and in Modania, it was no different. Bands of rebels from former governments, not content with the way things were progressing, were bent on disruption. They raided, stole, maimed or murdered anyone in their path in order to get what they wanted. After the Great War between the North and the South, policing the borders and dealing with arguments and disputes fell to the government of the South. Because they were the victors of that great battle, it was to them that this responsibility was given. It was only after very careful consideration that a selection, a party of twelve soldiers of high rank, was given the task of patrolling the land using organised routes. Their aims were to hear argument, settle claims and to award, where necessary, compensation. Their task also was to bring offenders to justice, create order within communities and to appoint leaders of men where necessary. As the years passed and the rule of law was obeyed, crime became less and less until what was left became manageable. As a result new communities grew and prospered. However, some of the more hardened of criminals passed prejudice from father to son in order to perpetuate ill-feeling.

It was this that culminated in a group of twenty renegades banding together. It was not long before these renegades heard tell of a treasure map being held by Aluen of Tybow. Scouts were sent out with instructions to find this Aluen of Tybow, and to deliver reports back to their ageing leader, a Northerner by the name of Syart who wanted the treasure map.

Aluen had first travelled towards the South, following the River Powle before heading westward on the coast road. He made good time and arrived at the village of Si-Port some nine days later. There had been an explosion of new towns and settlements over the past two or three decades, and as the populations expanded, more living areas and houses were needed. Si-Port, a town which bathed in the shadow of the Dete Beacons, was a fishing town whose harbour was constantly busy with incoming ships bringing their cargoes of fish and other goods to be sold at the harbour market. There was a certain aroma that lingered there, and it was one which Aluen found quite nauseating.

He was pleased when he found a place to set up camp near the outskirts of the town. News travelled fast in these populated areas and it was quickly known that there was an illusionist visiting the area, so Aluen was soon occupied giving demonstrations to the town's people. Some threw coins into a box in appreciation of the entertainment. Others donated fish and sea food or things they had made or grown.

Aluen was overwhelmed, he had not expected such a huge offering and thanked the town's people for their generosity. He arranged for some of the fish and sea foods to be packed in ice and taken by a merchant to his parents in the village of Tybow.

The merchant accepted some of the fish products as payment, which suited not only Aluen's pocket but his growing dislike of the aroma and the following of a large number of the town's pet population.

It was late in the evening when Aluen finally was able to set up his camp for the evening. He sat by a small campfire which he had managed to light in spite of the sea mist which filled the air. The smell of fish still permeated the atmosphere, and a number of luminous eyes watched from a distance. Even though Aluen had eaten his fill of the free food, there was still quite a lot left over so, thinking of the watching eyes, he occasionally threw a fish into the darkness. A frenzy of movement followed and luminous eyes could be seen bobbing up and down like so many fireflies dancing in the darkness. Aluen began to fall asleep. He was a little tired after his journey and his demonstrations of magic for the towns' folk. He welcomed the peace of the evening.

He had not been sleeping for long when he was abruptly awakened by a kick to his legs.

"Are you Aluen of Tybow?" The voice was gritty, with a regional dialect.

Aluen sat up and rubbed the sleep from his eyes. "Yes, he replied."

"Then you have something that belongs to us. It's a map, and we'll take your purse with it. Do I smell fish?" There was an evil grin on the faces of the two men who stood towering above Aluen. He quickly regained his composure.

"Are you sure you want to do this?" he bluffed. "I am after all a person who could call up demons to protect myself if needed." Then he pretended to chant an incantation in the hope that it would frighten the thieves away. The two men fell about laughing.

"You just give us the map and your money" said one. "We don't really want to hurt you but we will if we have to."

One of the men reached down to take a hold of Aluen's tunic, but he quickly stood up again apparently his eyes transfixed on something else. He seemed quite rigid with fear, and water began to darken the front of his leggings.

"Now go, and do not trouble me again" said Aluen. He was himself quite unaware that Cat stood behind him. The two men gathered enough courage to flee, and without another word they scrambled to safety.

"Quite easy if you know how to bluff," said Aluen to no one in particular. He picked up a large fish and threw it over his shoulder in mock triumph. When he heard the snap of large jaws and Cat walked into his field of vision, he sat bolt upright, not knowing what to do. The immense frame that was Cat moved towards the fire and sat down to devour the fish, making sure that afterwards she cleaned herself before lying down to purr her drum rolls of contentment. Aluen tried not to think about animals, especially large timber cats but this was not a dream, it was reality.

After some time had passed and Cat had not moved from the warmth of the fire, Aluen gathered up some courage. After all, he thought, the animal could have attacked him at any time but did not appear to want to. He carefully passed another fish which Cat took after sniffing it, then, gaining more confidence, Aluen made to stroke Cat's huge head. Cat ignored him. She was too busy enjoying the free meal.

"Well, I don't know how you came to be here with me, but you are welcome to stay as long as you like" he said. "There is only one provision, please don't eat me." Aluen smiled as he stroked Cat's fur. Cat looked up at Aluen, blinked, and returned to her fish supper.

The two thieves, who should have simply reported seeing Aluen of Tybow, were totally baffled as to how they came to be in a cesspit at Dronecet Castle, even more so when they realised that they were miles away from where they should be. An elderly gentleman chuckled to himself from his concealment in the shadows.

As morning dawned a mist hugged the ground, swirling around the trees and bushes like an ocean of cooling steam. Aluen woke up shivering as he remembered the evening before when the Timber Cat had appeared. Was it a dream? Did he really see a Timber Cat or was he imagining the visit from the abnormally huge creature? Had he made it appear with his pretend incantations? He looked around to see if there were any visible signs of a visit, but there were none at all. He pushed the thoughts to one side and made up the dying campfire before cooking himself a breakfast of… fish.

It was no more than one hour before Aluen was on the move again. He had dampened the campfire to prevent the fire spreading to the trees and was pleased to leave the smell of fish behind. The mist began to clear as he headed southward on the coast road. The sun began to warm the day and Aluen was happy.

Master Errol gently knocked at the door which led to his parents' bedchamber. His mother, the Lady

Elanor, who was already dressed and was busy tidying the rooms, answered the door. Lady Elanor had at one time been a woman of great beauty and age, although showing its wearying effect, had not altogether run amok over her fine features. She held herself proudly, a slender-framed woman who commanded the respect of all who met her. Her hair was worn long and, like her husband's, it was blonde. A few grey strands appeared to highlight it and give a steadfast maturity to her looks. She was, as expected, a well-spoken woman, and had at her disposal a huge vocabulary and command of languages both spoken, and signed. This, combined with a lifetime of learned knowledge, made her a formidable opponent in debate and a treasure in conversation.

"Excuse me Mother," Master Errol bowed as a sign of respect. "There is a person visiting the castle and he has petitioned to see Father. He says that his name is Birch."

"Birch?" called Lord Torran, who had been listening.

"Yes Father." Master Errol peeped through the gap in the door where the hinges met with the door post and saw his father hurriedly dressing.

"Elanor, its Birch." Lord Torran was excited, and it showed as he fumbled about with his robes.

"Yes dear, so I have just been informed."

"But it's… *the* Birch," he insisted as he was pulling on a boot and hopping around the room in the process.

"Yes I know, husband. Now get dressed properly, and have a wash before you meet this visitor. I will entertain Master Birch until your arrival."

"Yes, Elanor," said Lord Torran submissively.

Lady Elanor accepted Master Errol's arm as they walked along the passage and told him not to smirk at his father's misfortune of being nagged at. She confided that wives have a duty to nag in order to keep their husbands in line. After descending two flights of stone steps, they arrived at the main hall where Birch stood waiting. A huge fire blazed away in an open hearth which kept the huge hall warm.

"Master Birch," called Master Errol as he and his mother walked towards him. "May I present to you my mother, the Lady Elanor?"

"Indeed, I am honoured to make your acquaintance at last, Lady Elanor," said Birch, bowing respectfully. "I have kept up with the news and events although I have not, until this moment, presented myself before you."

Lady Elanor gave Birch a warm hug as if they were old friends and Birch took an instant liking to this, the most welcoming of all the women he had met.

"It is I who should be honoured, Master Birch. It

is not often that we are visited by a person such as yourself. You are a person of great skill and command of the arts. It is a subject that I have read about often and have a keen interest in, although I do not have the gift of producing such wonders as you. I am, however, very knowledgeable in regard to the uses of plant life in the treatment and recovery of injury and ill health. Tell me, are there many with such knowledge?"

"A few, my lady but…"

"Please, Master Birch," interrupted Lady Elanor. "Call me Elanor."

"Yes… er… Elanor," Birch was slightly taken aback by Lady Elanor's openness. "The study takes years, with little benefit I might add. There are some religious organisations with the time to study, but, alas, not many others have the kind of dedication needed to succeed in this field."

"That is such a shame, Master Birch. Errol, would you be a dear and go to the kitchen? Ask if some breakfast could be arranged for our guest. I presume that you will join us, Master Birch?"

"An invitation I would be a fool to refuse, Elanor."

"First name terms already?" came a voice descending the stairs.

Birch watched as Lord Torran, now with a slight limp, walked towards him. For a moment the two men looked at each other and took in the effects of the passage of time. They nodded their approval of the changes, then, without another word, they came together and warmly clasped hands and embraced.

"It has been a long, long time my friend," said Lord Torran. "How is Cat?"

"She is still as big as ever. The years have treated you well, Torran, and I might add, what a delightful and knowledgeable companion you have in the Lady Elanor. No regrets?"

"None Birch, I have no regrets whatsoever. I have a good woman who has given me a fine boy. I am content. Now tell me, what brings you to the castle after such a long leave of absence? It must be something of importance to arrive at such an early hour."

"You can talk over breakfast," interrupted Lady Elanor as the kitchen staff arrived with plates of meat, fruit, bread, honey and wine.

The three men obeyed a little sheepishly as they sat at a long table that was usually reserved for banquets and, while they enjoyed the freshly-prepared breakfast, Birch explained to Lady Elanor that it had been his decision to stay away from the more populated areas for so long. If he had been, for instance, a regular visitor to the castle, then people being people, they would be forever asking him to perform small feats of magic, of actual magic. That he would eventually become noticed as different from the others. He would become the object of ridicule, a freak, and magic was never meant to be for the amusement of the inquisitive. People would then try to buy services, or they would ask for just a little silver, or maybe gold. They would offer position and wealth and then get angry when refused. No, magic was almost sacred to Birch in that he would only use it when danger threatened, or to prevent a catastrophe. He then explained the reasons for his visit, that someone not known to him had used strong magic. He enquired if Lord Zelfen was still a prisoner in The Watch, or maybe a stranger to the land had been seen, a stranger who, like himself, had the power to use magic. Lord Torran assured him that if Lord Zelfen had escaped, then the night guard would have informed him immediately.

Birch was lost in thought for a while, and during this brief period he sent his thoughts out to Cat in the hope that she would respond. For some reason he found this difficult. He could not make a connection and this began to worry him further.

"I'm not sure what's going on" said Birch. He was pacing the room and was visibly agitated. "First of all I hear real magic being performed, and now I have lost contact with Cat. I shall have to investigate further on this matter."

Lord Torran was the first to reply. "Can we be of any assistance?"

"Thank you for your concern, Torran, but not on this occasion. Sometimes, as you yourself are aware my friend, my modes of travel together with my actions could be most disturbing to the unenlightened."

"As you wish my friend, but we will be ready to help under any circumstance if needed. Who knows what situations tomorrow might present. For instance, Karl might get out of bed early for a change."

"I heard that, fishface!" Lord Karl entered the room with his son, Master Terance. A huge smile beamed when he saw Birch, and Master Terance looked on inquisitively. Lord Karl had also married, but tragedy had befallen the union. His lady had fallen ill during her pregnancy, and had passed away during childbirth. Lord Karl was heartbroken at this great loss, but support was at hand. Lady Elanor was first to offer her services and accepted the charge that she would tend and care for Master Terance during his tender years. It followed that he and Master Errol became inseparable as youngsters and shared a brotherly togetherness that none could counter.

However, the passing years had taken their toll. He had not quite come to terms with the death of his wife so early in their marriage, and his hair, slightly receding, had turned from the deepest black to mottled grey. Like his father Lord Brin at his age, Lord Karl had gained a few pounds, and the lines on his face told their own story. Lord Brin of Tezz had passed away some years earlier and it was a trying time, especially for Lord Torran who missed his friend more than most. Time however had healed the mental scars that followed the loss and memories became treasured in the minds of those who knew him. The breakfast continued for some considerable time as the tales continued to flow, then, thanking Lady Elanor for her hospitality, and shaking hands with his breakfast companions, Birch made his apologies and took his leave.

He's worried." Lord Torran broke the silence after Birch's departure.

"I'm sure he will be able to look after himself," remarked lady Elanor.

"Maybe we should tighten the security arrangements just in case," suggested Lord Karl.

"Maybe.....maybe," Lord Torran was deep in thought.

CHAPTER THREE

Syart was angry. It showed on his hawk-like features. It showed when he stomped around the room with complete disregard for anything, or anyone. Syart was a heavily-built man of medium height. His stooping posture and the way he positioned his hands on his hips reminded his fellow renegades of a magpie, a talking point in Syart's absence. His black, matted hair streaked with grey and coupled with a prominent hooked nose completed the picture.

"So, he has escaped?" The words fell slowly from his thin lips with venom that everyone understood. "Aluen of Tybow, a mere boy, has eluded two of my most trusted lieutenants. Two men who were supposed to be the best in their field have failed, two men whom I sent out and who promised results." Syart raised his voice so much that his screeching began to resemble the ravings of a maniac. "The message I received reads that this boy, Aluen of

Tybow, can call demons at will. Demons. Demons!" he shouted across the room.

This made the assembled renegades begin to fear for their lives. It was known that Syart had often made examples of those who had failed him. "A big black cat with a head as big as a bull, must have been terrifying, if they actually saw one. More likely they had seen the bottom of a bottle. Why did they not report to me like I asked? Can no one obey orders anymore? Right!" he shouted as he turned once more to face his mismatched group of men. "Four of you travel to the West. Four more of you I want to travel to the south-west with a single purpose. I want this Aluen of Tybow, this demon maker and finder of my map. I want this map in my possession without delay. Demon-maker. Pah!"

Syart's renegades, terrified of what might become of them if they missed any more opportunities of obtaining the map, scampered out of the low building, took to their horses and galloped away towards their respective destinations. After a short while of pacing up and down, Syart himself took to horse and followed.

★ ★ ★

The snow-capped mountains of the Dete Beacons

towered into the early morning sky. Aluen had remained at the same campsite for almost six days. He was captivated by the sheer beauty of his surroundings and stood in awe of the spectacular skies during the twilight of the early dawn. To Aluen, the diamond dust, minute reflective particles of cosmic ice, created a magic of their own. Huge triangles of multi-coloured lights were formed and pointed upwards from the horizon. He had just sat down by his camp-fire after watching the spectacle when someone called his name.

"Aluen? Aluen of Tybow?"

"I am proud to bear that name. How can I help you, sir?"

"Well Aluen of Tybow, I have ridden hard and travelled quite extensively to meet with you," said Syart as he approached the camp.

"You have, and why do I deserve this honour?"

"Well, my fortunate friend," said Syart with a smile that showed rows of blackened teeth. "It appears that you have some property that may belong to me. A map, yes a map. It was lost during my recent travels when I visited a mystic fair at Dronecet Castle," he lied. "I wonder if you still have the map about your person?"

"I'm afraid that you have me at a loss, sir. I have no map." Aluen had told Syart the truth in this statement.

"No map?" Syart's anger flared for a moment but

he kept it in check. Realising that he would accomplish nothing by a show of anger, his wicked smile returned. "But I was informed - er, notified - that you had indeed found such a parchment."

"Oh, do you mean this parchment?" Aluen produced the parchment scroll from his sack and showed Syart who, without hesitation, snatched it from Aluen's hands and examined it in detail.

"This isn't a map!" Syart was angry and still studying the words. "It's only words. Is this the only parchment that you found?"

"Yes it is. I have already told you that I haven't got a map."

"Well this isn't the map that I lost, but tell me, what do you think these words mean?" Syart's crafty grin betrayed that, had the parchment been a map, he would have most certainly tried to steal it. As the parchment only revealed words, he had to find someone who had the capability of deciphering them so as to discover their meaning.

"I don't really know what the words mean either, but I am going to find out if I can."

"I'm sure you will." Syart put his arm around Aluen in a gesture of friendship. "Maybe I can help. Come, I'll take you to my humble dwelling where we might find some way of unlocking the secret together." Syart supposed that Aluen knew more than he was prepared to disclose at that time, and he was not about to let him go - not just yet. "Here, let me help you pack your things," he said while nervously looking about in case anyone was watching. The last thing he wanted at this time was interference from anyone, or anything. He was still cautious after hearing the tales of demons and strange occurrences.

"That's very kind of you."

"Yes it is, isn't it?"

Little did Aluen know the ways of renegades and the lengths to which they would go to achieve their aims. Life in the village where Aluen had grown to manhood was honest and simple, and so he put his trust in Syart. However, he did have reservations and he was extremely observant. He noticed that Syart had difficulty in understanding words and had not appreciated the misspelling of the word 'SEE'.

As they travelled away from the coast, Aluen became increasingly uneasy with his travelling companion, so much so that it occurred to him that he might attempt to escape his circumstances, but on reflection he considered that it would be a bad mistake to do so. Syart would certainly have become violent and Aluen was not a capable person in this field. He decided to wait for a better opportunity, an opportunity that would not involve getting hurt, or worse.

When they had travelled a considerable distance inland across the desert, Syart, who was a naturally cautious person, asked Aluen about the use of magic, and if he was any good at performing it. Aluen answered by saying that he was just an illusionist, not a magician. Syart seemed somewhat relieved, but posed another question.

"Someone told me that you can summon demons," he said, warily.

Aluen was defensive. If Syart knew about the last attempted robbery, he might well be in league with the renegades. It appeared to be the only explanation. "Well I might have created an illusion from time to time" he said. It's nothing really but what I try to do is called suggestive power."

"Suggestive power?"

"Yes. I suggest that someone can see something, and they do. They create the illusion themselves, but it doesn't happen very often."

"Could these illusions ever hurt anyone?"

"No of course they couldn't. They are after all just figments of the imagination." Aluen determined that Syart had little knowledge about such matters because he, Aluen, was talking in riddles that sounded about right.

They camped that evening atop a small rise in the sands and Aluen, after building a campfire out of discarded wood found on his journey, offered Syart some salted fish, the last piece he had. For himself he decided upon cheese and fruit. It made a wonderful change. Syart was thankful, or he appeared to be, because it seemed that Aluen had given up his main meal. Little did he know that Aluen was getting a little tired of fish and was quite pleased that the last piece had gone.

Conversation dwindled as the night crept slowly across the land and the flames of the camp fire danced their dance in the cooling night air. Syart was not an outdoor person, especially during the hours of darkness. He was jittery and the eerie sounds of the desert night-life added to his nervousness. Aluen, on the other hand, was quite used to the open air and was soon bedded down. He was almost asleep when Syart leapt from the log he was sitting on.

"Who's there? Who's there?" he called.

"What's the matter?" Aluen awoke and began to look around.

"I'm positive that I saw something. I thought I saw two green eyes staring at me but I may have been mistaken."

"The desert sands playing tricks, or maybe fireflies. Go to sleep."

"Maybe I will."

Aluen instinctively knew that the Timber Cat had

followed them. What Syart had thought he'd imagined was something very real, something very, very dangerous to some but a playful kitten to others. 'Maybe she wanted some more fish' thought Aluen. He couldn't think at that time of any other reason why the Timber Cat should follow them.

Slowly he drifted off to sleep, happy in the knowledge that something, probably friendly, was close at hand. Syart eventually fell asleep, but it was a restless sleep punctuated by visions of green eyes. No matter how he tried to dismiss the visions, he could not make them go away. He decided that it was purely his imagination and considered that Aluen might be involved in creating his condition.

Eventually he sat up, and with his blanket wrapped round his shoulders, he built up the camp-fire and waited until dawn. It seemed like an age before the rim of the sun peeped over the distant horizon, but it was a cold sun. The unusually warm autumn was nearing its unstoppable climax as wintry winds swept the landscape with promises of still colder times to come. Syart shivered, and although the camp fire was blazing sending sparks in all directions, the warmth it was producing was being taken away along with the wind. There were dark semicircles around Syart's eyes caused by the lack of sleep. His cheeks were drawn in and his hooked nose, besides being red at the tip, had needed wiping more than once since the onset of dawn.

Aluen stirred from his slumber and stretched. He was used to the cold, as most country people are. Helping his father on numerous occasions during the winter, he had got used to the conditions. He looked up towards Syart, turned his head and sniggered to himself. He found Syart's discomfort most amusing.

"Good morning," he said, trying desperately to hide his amusement. "What we need is some nice hot broth." He folded his blanket and stored it in a dry area before taking out a large iron pot into which he poured water from his supplies. Setting it onto the fire, he added bones and vegetables. "This will keep out the chill" he said.

Syart said nothing. He just sat by the fire and shivered.

"Not used to the cold weather?" Aluen smiled.

"One more word young man, just one more word!" shouted Syart, with an emphasis that suggested that a volcano was about to erupt. But for the fact that Aluen had a cart and could only travel slowly, especially across sand, he would have been more than half way home at this stage and a lot warmer.

"I'll leave you to your own company if you wish." Aluen was still smiling, which tore at Syart's nerves.

"No no," interrupted Syart. "Forgive my outburst.

I have had a restless night."

"So it seems."

'When your usefulness is past,' thought Syart. 'I will take the greatest of pleasure in ripping out your heart and feeding it to the rats.' Aluen could almost hear the thought so nothing more was said until the food was ready to serve. The marrow from the bones and the vegetables made a welcoming meal. Even Syart had to agree that he thoroughly enjoyed it, 'shame that I have to kill the chef when the secrets of the parchment are revealed,' he thought. After the meal and after packing everything onto the cart they continued their journey. The wind was still biting with its coldness, but Aluen was enjoying it and began to sing as they travelled.

"Will you shut up!" screamed Syart who was feeling miserable.

Aluen, himself quite warm being used to the cold, just smiled which really angered Syart.

'He's using the power of suggestion,' he thought, 'but I'll not give in to it. He can try all he wants to but he will not catch me out.'

As a matter of fact, Aluen was doing no such thing. He was just being his normally happy self, more so because Syart was miserable. He did think that maybe, just maybe when the time was right, he could use this to his advantage. He remembered that he had seen this power of suggestion demonstrated some time in the past when he had visited a display of magic. The magician had called it hypnotism. Not that Aluen wanted to demonstrate this style of entertainment, but the knowledge of how it worked might indeed come in handy.

★ ★ ★

"There's another one, my lord." The soldier stood to attention, but with a slight grin on his face.

"There's another one in the same place?" Lord Tamur was puzzled.

"There's another two actually, my lord,"

"Good heavens, that's… let me see now…"

"Seven so far, my lord."

"Yes, seven. Is there something going on that we should know about? I mean, what's the attraction? What is their state of mind? Do they appear to be normal?"

"I have no idea what the attraction might be, my lord. They appear to have all their faculties, with the exception that they seem to be scared sh… they look worried, my lord."

"Is diving into cesspits something to do with some new-style religion? Is it a new skin preparation?"

"I shouldn't think so my lord. Shall I have them

cleaned up?" The soldier could hardly contain his mirth.

"Yes, and make them do some work for a few days. We can't have people diving into our cesspit. Just think what it would be like if everyone did the same."

"I shall put them to work in the gardens, my lord."

"Yes, and I shall go and inform Lord Edmund of these strange occurrences. He likes to be kept informed of developments, and this is certainly something that makes the brain itch."

"It certainly does, my lord." The soldier awaited dismissal.

"Oh, of course," Lord Tamur was lost in thought for a moment. "You may go about your duties."

"By your leave, my lord." The soldier turned smartly. Still holding back the laughter, he went to help the unfortunate wretches.

The guardroom was a plain, brick building of no great size, but it was adequate for the needs of the castle. Inside there were holding cells, but apart from the torches mounted on the walls which provided light, there was little by way of decoration. A large desk and a few chairs and benches provided basic furnishings and an open fire provided the warmth.

Two men stood before the soldier who had returned from his meeting with Lord Tamur. They were trying to give a description of their ordeal but not without some difficulty.

"It's true, I tell you," said one of the would-be thieves. "We were just walking toward an encampment. It was very late in the evening and it was bitterly cold, and we thought to seek warmth by the camp fire. Maybe we would be allowed something to eat if the occupier was feeling generous. The next moment we felt strange. There was a kind of wind and strange lights. When we came to our senses we found ourselves in this condition."

"Do you think it would be nearer the truth to say that you went out last night, helped yourselves to some ale, lost you way and fell into the cesspit while in a drunken stupor?" suggested the soldier.

"No no no. We were miles away from this castle when it happened," said the other thief. "It was as my friend here described. First we were hoping for some comfort by an open fire, maybe something to eat. Then we felt a little dizzy. I thought I had blacked out. The next thing I knew I was up to my neck in your cesspit along with my friend here."

"Have you got both your hands?" asked the soldier.

"What do you mean? Of course we have both our hands. What kind of question is that?"

"These are strange times, my friend, and you are not the only ones who have been fished out of the cesspit. The first person swore blind that his hand was missing although it was in plain sight. All right, get yourselves cleaned up. You will find some robes have been provided, and when you have finished you will report back to me in this guard room. I will find some work for you to do. It will repay the kindness of the lord of this castle in allowing you to clean yourselves, and for the provision of some clean clothes."

"Work?" the poor wretches looked dejected.

"Yes, work. I'll be back in a short while, and don't think of trying to get away without repaying the lord's kindness. He would take a very dim view of such an action."

The soldier then left and hurried across to the main hall where Lord Tamur stood in front of a huge open-grated fireplace.

"My lord?"

"Yes, soldier?"

"I'm afraid that it is the same as the last two occasions, my lord."

"Do you mean to say that they have no idea how they managed to get where they were?"

"That's about the size of it, my lord."

"All right, you may go about your duties."

"With your leave, my lord." The soldier marched quickly away.

Lord Tamur thought for a while before leaving the main hall. He walked slowly toward a low building which was separated from the other buildings within the castle walls and surrounded by a small but adequate garden. This was the house of his father and mother, Lord Edmund and his wife of many years, Jaelia. They had both retired from public life, and wished only to enjoy their last few years without the burden of management and paperwork, without the day-to-day decision-making, and with the knowledge that they could leave at a moment's notice to go wherever they wished without any duties preventing it.

"My pardon, Father," said Lord Tamur as he entered the reception area of the house. "I have an enigma that I cannot solve and I beg your assistance with it."

Lord Edmund was of stocky build, but despite his age he was still strong of arm, and with a quickness that would not normally be associated with one so old.

"Well my boy, out with it. Jaelia, bring some refreshments please. Are we too old that we forget our manners?"

Jaelia, Lord Edmund's wife, was without a doubt a blessing in the way that she cared for her husband. For him she had kept a fine figure, and if it were not for the tell-tale signs of greying hair tied neatly in a bun at the back, she could easily be mistaken for someone quite a few years younger.

"Don't fuss, Edmund," she called from another room. "Refreshments take time to prepare. I will be with you shortly."

"Shorty?" laughed Edmund.

"I said I will be with you short–ly. Wash your ears out, Edmund."

"Be careful when you marry," remarked Lord Edmund to his son. "This one will nag me to death."

"I heard that," Jaelia entered the reception room carrying a tray on which stood wine and hot biscuits. She smiled at her son. "Don't keep him too long because it's almost time to change him," she laughed.

"Get away with you, woman." Edmund smiled and gave her a friendly pat on the rump as she returned to her household duties. "Now my son, what is so important that you need my input to solve a problem? You are quite capable of solving problems yourself."

"Father, this one is very strange. So far seven people have been rescued from the castle cesspit. The first one was just a few weeks ago and last night there were two."

"Oh dear!"

"The thing is, not one of them could remember how they got there."

"Probably had an evening out, drank too much and fell in."

"No Father. It appears that only one of the seven was in the vicinity of the castle at the time. The rest were, or so they said, miles away from here. One minute they were in one place, the next minute they were in the castle cesspit."

"Why would anyone want to translocate?"

Lord Tamur was about to answer the question when he noticed that his father appeared to be in a trance. He was as memories of former times came flooding back to him.

"Are you all right, Father?"

"Yes, yes of course I'm all right. Bring the latest visitors to me. I would ask them some questions."

"Yes, Father."

Lord Tamur returned to the guard room, where the two travellers now looked presentable, having taken a bath and dressed in the clean clothes provided. "You two," he said to the travellers. "Come with me. My father would ask you some further questions, and pay due respect to him."

"Yes, my lord," they chorused.

The two travellers were led by Lord Tamur across the main parade ground to his father's house. Respectfully he knocked on the door before entering and ushered the two travellers into a side room before repeating his orders to pay due respect to his father. They stood with their hands clasped in front of them, not quite knowing what to expect, or what their fate might be. After what seemed to be an age, Lord Edmund came into the room carrying a tray of refreshments.

"You two certainly appear to have had a bad night. Here, help yourselves. Drink, eat and be refreshed," he said.

The two men were shocked at the unexpected civility of this lord and thanked him profusely for the hospitality.

"Tell me," began Lord Edmund as he gazed out from a small window at his well-kept gardens. "I am somewhat bewildered by the tale that has been told to me regarding the situation which you found yourselves in last evening. It appears to me a most remarkable thing to have happened to two sober, upstanding and honest people." The word 'honest' was emphasised and Lord Edmund looked at them directly with his steel-blue, penetrating eyes. The two travellers swallowed hard.

Lord Edmund continued, trying not to laugh. "I have been led to believe that you two were some miles away before suddenly finding yourselves in the castle cesspit."

"That is more or less what happened, sire. One minute we were hoping to spend a night before a nice warm fire. Maybe if we were lucky we would have been offered something to eat. Then the next minute we were in the sh…"

"We were in the castle cesspit up to our necks," interrupted the other traveller.

"And did you by any chance happen to meet with anyone on your journey? For instance, did you speak with the person at the camp site? What did he look like?"

"He was a young man, sire. He had a horse and cart."

"And was the young man alone?"

"As far as we could tell he was, my lord".

"All right you may go," said Lord Edmund. Then almost as an afterthought he said, "And try to lead an honest existence from now on."

"Begging your pardon, my lord."

A glance from those blue eyes told them not to say anything else. "Tamur, give these two men some tasks to perform. It will help pay for the hospitality they have received."

"Yes Father."

An ageing flint had sparked a memory in Lord Edmund's mind, a spark that had travelled through history, freeing itself from the frozen winds of time and bringing memories flooding back, memories of Lord Karl and Lord Torran, of Master Elio and Master Birch; memories of pain, of anger, of happiness and of sadness. He remembered his former servant, Tamur, and a tear formed in the corner of his eye. Such was this servant's devotion, even unto death, that Edmund had named his own son after him. He had often visited Lord Karl and Lord Torran, though not as often as he would have liked, and when he mentioned that events had spurred his decision to visit again, Jaelia was thrilled. Jaelia was extremely fond of the two lords, and any excuse to visit was seized upon, even if only to hear Masters Errol and Derik call each other rude names. She began the preparations immediately, sending orders to catering staff, supply staff and personnel. Guards were told to make ready for a long-awaited journey to Castle Tezz.

The winds were blowing around the fields in little eddies, biting, chapping bare flesh into red sores. Remnants of leaves danced about on the hard ground. Naked trees offered little shelter for winter birds. They looked down accusingly at Aluen and Syart as they slowly progressed through the cold, dry wind. They had travelled only a short distance from the desert, mainly due to the speed of Aluen's cart, when, in the distance, four riders came into view. They halted and waited for the riders to approach.

"Syart" one of the men called as they drew nearer.

The men were almost unrecognisable because of

the layers of fur clothing they had wrapped themselves in as a protection against the cold wind.

"Of course it's me," growled Syart, shivering. "You don't think that for one minute I'd leave such an important task entirely to a bunch of no-hopers like you, do you? While you probably stopped to refresh yourselves with country mead, cheap wine and the pleasures of the flesh, I have made a few discreet enquiries and found our quarry almost a full day before you thought to look properly."

"Excuse me," called Aluen when he heard the word 'quarry'.

"Be quiet, boy," replied Syart in a vicious tone as he continued to ridicule his men. "Do you not realise that we could have lost this young idiot if it were not for me?"

The situation now became much clearer to Aluen. This Syart character was interested only in the scroll, and once its secrets had been fully revealed, with him to help as a translator, Syart would have no further use for him. What would happen to him then? He had a fairly good idea. He could not execute a quick getaway with his present mode of transport, it was too slow and he would easily be caught. Besides which, Syart still had the scroll and Aluen was not about to leave without it. He would have to hope that a chance to escape would present itself sooner, rather than later.

They continued travelling until the daylight began to fade, and when it became too dark to travel, Syart ordered that a camp for the night be made.

"Watch our young friend," said Syart to his men. "He can read, and I'm almost positive that he knows more than he has already told me."

The mountain region and the desert were behind them now, and the land before them was given over to farming. As a result there was little by way of fuel for a decent campfire. Syart, with no sense of regret, ordered Aluen's boxes and cart to be used as firewood. Aluen's protests were ignored. His pleading fell on deaf ears as his possessions, invaluable to him, were broken up one by one to feed the campfire. Aluen was devastated. He sat with his head in his hands as piece by piece, the fire consumed all of his hard-earned equipment to give a little warmth to a gang of renegades. His food store was emptied. His fresh water had been consumed. He felt totally frustrated that he could do little about the situation. He screamed at the renegades.

"Well I hope that you don't want me to help you with your quest to discover the secret of the scroll, because I won't" he said. He suddenly realised that in his temper, he had said too much. He fell silent.

"Ah! So there is a secret to these words. I had thought as much." Syart tapped the scroll against his palms. "And you, my young companion, will help me." His mood changed and his face flushed with anger. "Believe me, Aluen. You will help or I will feed your living entrails to the pigs while you watch."

"Is that the map?" asked one of the renegades.

"Is that the map? Is that the map?" mocked Syart. "There is no map. Do you think for one moment he would still be alive if that were the case, if it was that simple?" He held up the scroll. "This is a parchment containing words. Words within which a secret of treasure is concealed, a secret that, mark my words, I will find with the help of our young friend." He smiled an evil, black-toothed smile, and looked directly at the now frightened Aluen. Aluen quickly hid his feelings, tried to build a little bravado and asked to look at the scroll again.

"That's the spirit. I might even spare your miserable life if you help to solve the mystery." Syart winked at his men.

Aluen thought again of escape, but there were five against him, and where would he go before Syart and his men caught up with him? He slowly unrolled the scroll, lowered his head and began to chant. He remembered doing this once before, when it had appeared to frighten some thieves into running away. He hoped that it would work this time as well.

"It will not work, my boy." Syart was enjoying this, but his men were not so sure.

"Do you think for one moment that I would be travelling alone, unprotected and against such as you?" said Aluen. He was trying to put on a brave face.

"Oh dear me, now let me recall an earlier conversation for a moment, ah yes, now I remember what you told me, illusion created by the mind. Do you take me for a fool, Aluen? You can't hurt us with your make-believe magic."

Aluen suddenly and regretfully realised his mistake in telling Syart about the effect of illusions in their earlier conversations. For once he felt empty and resigned to his fate.

"Well, well," continued Syart. "Are we now lost for words? The intelligent Master Aluen of Tybow!" he mocked. "Come to think about it, you are not the only person in the land who can read, are you? There are greater scholars, and far less expensive ones. To be quite honest, for once in my life, I don't think that is it necessary for us to continue this journey together, young Master Aluen."

"Does that mean I can go?" asked a hopeful Aluen.

Syart and his men almost fell about laughing. Then Syart's face changed slowly to an expression of deep concern. "Oh no no, young Master Aluen, you will be staying here, so to speak. The parchment must remain a secret that I'm not about to share with anyone. I don't think it is necessary for you to continue living, is what I am saying".

Syart's four renegade companions had gathered around their leader and begun to discuss who would have the pleasure of dispatching the now nervous Aluen when, noticing something strange, one of the renegades nudged Syart and pointed to his left. In the darkness of the surrounding fields two luminous green eyes, eyes that appeared to be too far apart, watched the group whilst moving closer towards where they stood. They saw a hooded figure, ageing by the look of a long white beard which could be clearly seen in the flickering firelight, and beside it something huge and black.

"Well well well," said Syart. "Is this one of your Illusions? It's very good, very good. The eyes are maybe a little wide apart though. Take no notice." He turned to his men. "Illusions are created in an attempt to frighten us. They cannot actually hurt anyone, besides there are five of us, right?" He held out his arm and swept it in an arc as though to emphasise his words. However, when he turned around there were only three other men.

"Where did the other man go? Was he frightened of an illusion? Did he run away like a scared rabbit?"

"We don't know, Syart," replied one of the three remaining men. "He was standing with us a moment ago."

"Well I'll have no more of it. Young Master Aluen is trying to make us look like fools," said another renegade. Drawing his sword, and with a consenting nod from Syart, he walked purposely toward a cowering Aluen.

The next few seconds were difficult to comprehend. The supposed illusion came to life, and a huge black mass fell upon the advancing renegade. It was as though part of the night itself had become detached and fallen briefly before disappearing once more to join the rest of the blackness. The fallen renegade lay in his final death throes, his injuries too terrible to contemplate. Aluen could only look on and feel the dying man's terror. He was thankful that he had not been on the receiving end of the renegade's sword.

"I thought you said illusions could not hurt," muttered one of the men.

"Illusions are not always what they appear to be" said a voice from the darkness. "Take to your horse and cart, Master Aluen. You must continue your quest."

"But they have destroyed all that I had," wailed Aluen to the mysterious voice in the darkness.

"Have you still no faith?, you who chant the names of the three gods each time you find yourself in difficulties? Do you not understand that they do listen and they do hear you? They are aware of your plight," said the voice.

Aluen looked into the darkness with a question forming on his lips, but before he could utter one word, he saw a line of multi-coloured star shapes appear. He watched in wonder as they travelled through the blackness. They approached him and soared up through the night sky, then, beginning to spiral downwards, they fell onto the campfire. The fire appeared to explode, and in one final display of bright glittering colour, it disappeared and was replaced with Aluen's cart. The cart was complete with his illusion boxes and tricks; his food and water supplies were there as well. Two oil lamps were the only addition, placed on each side to give light.

Aluen stood there amazed. His complete and utter joy could be seen as tears of thankfulness which fell unheeded from his smiling eyes. He turned to say something, but the figure had disappeared. Cat however had not, and came walking into the campsite to stand by him.

Syart and his remaining two men appeared to have fled, although their final destination wasn't exactly as they had planned. It is said, however, that a sight-seeing tour of Dronecet Castle at this time of year does wonders for the education. Of course this would depend upon whether or not you were a student of human by-products.

"Well my friend, we meet again," said Aluen as

he ran his fingers through Cat's thick fur. "What I would give for a friend and travelling companion such as you."

"Quite a lot, I would imagine." Master Elio stepped out from the shadows and into the lights of the lamps. Aluen didn't know whether to laugh, cry, bow or prostrate himself.

"Master Elio! I... I am indebted and I apologise for my misgivings, but I am thrilled to find real magic. I knew it existed, I just knew it. Can you show me some more?"

"Master Aluen, magic is not a toy to be used to entertain. It is a gift that has responsibilities attached. I leave the entertainment to illusionists such as yourself, and you are a very good one, I must admit."

"You have watched my performances?"

"For quite a while, my young friend. I have been watching your progress, and keeping you out of trouble."

"You are protecting me? Master Elio I don't quite understand. Maybe if you could explain a few..."

Master Elio held up his hand for Aluen to be silent. "The ways of the world are in themselves an enigma at times, young Master Aluen. We all do as we must without question, because we know what we do is the right thing at the right time. No one can explain this, it just is. If you fall foul of any others with ill-intention on your remaining journey, have no fear, for friends will be close at all times."

Before Aluen could enquire further, Master Elio faded amid an array of silver stars and was gone. Cat lingered for a while before she too bounded away and melted into the darkness. Silence followed. Aluen found the events of that evening confusing, difficult to believe and even more so to understand. "Why me?" he shouted into the darkness.

There was only silence. He sat by the remains of his camp fire and smiled because few people would believe that he had a friend in the form of an eight-foot Timber Cat. No-one would believe that he was a friend of Master Elio, a centuries-old master magician, besides his father of course. He laughed out loud at the thought, and as he looked up into the night sky, he smiled and offered silent thanks. He imagined that he saw the gods smiling back; or was it really his imagination?

Dawn began to move slowly across the land, the sky a misty grey colour. The blackness of the night gave way to another cold morning. Sharp, icy winds danced and swirled across the farmlands, leaving a cold whiteness tipping the upper edges of the ploughed soil, bushes and grass. The intricate patterns of gossamer threads that formed spiders' webs looked like lace decorations.

Aluen shivered as he climbed onto his cart. He sat for a moment's reflection before spurring his horse into action to continue his journey southward. All that was left in that place was a shallow grave.

★ ★ ★

Preparations were still being made at Dronecet Castle for the intended journey to Castle Tezz when a guardsman begged entry to Lord Tamur's office. Lord Tamur and Lord Edmund were still discussing the business that needed attention during the short period in which they would be away from the castle. They proposed that the Captain of the Guard, a well-respected and trusted officer, would take control of the castle business during their absence, and having accepted the responsibility, he was fully briefed.

"Excuse me, my lords," said the guardsman, quite impatiently.

The Captain of the Guard, a little unnerved by the guardsman's manner, strode over to him. "Your impatience in this place is unwarranted, soldier. What is so important that you disturb us in conference? Can't it wait?"

"Sir, I apologise, but I'm afraid that we have some more... er... visitors, sir."

"Not the cesspit again?"

"I'm afraid so, sir."

"How many are there this time?"

"Four we have counted, sir."

"Four?" the Captain put his head in his hands in disbelief.

"Yes sir, but one of them is, I am pleased to report, the renegade Syart, a man we have been trying to apprehend for some considerable time."

"What is their story? Is it the same as the others?"

"Sir, even I have difficulty in believing their story this time. They say that the night fell on one of their companions. Then a horse and cart they had appropriated, the cart and its contents they claim to have burned for firewood due to the condition, suddenly and without explanation reappeared like new and without a burn mark on it. Then they mentioned something about coloured lights and an oversized Timber Cat. It's all a little confusing, sir."

"Very well, you did the right thing in coming to see me, but remember to pay due respect next time. Carry out the usual procedure. Clean them down and give them fresh clothing. We will be along to see them shortly."

"By your leave, sir." The soldier returned to his slightly baffling duties.

The discussion in Lord Tamur's office lasted a few more minutes before all the business had been finalised. "I think the main points have been covered, Captain," announced Lord Tamur. "We will not be away for too long at Castle Tezz, and Lord Edmund and I are convinced that you will be able to cope with the finer points. One more thing, you will need to organise some men to gather wood for the winter store."

"It will be as you wish, my lord."

"Right, let's go and see our new arrivals."

The Captain of the Guard led the way as he, Lord Tamur and his father, Lord Edmund, walked over to the gatehouse where Syart and his renegades were being held in secure rooms. They appeared to be a little happier now that they had cleaned themselves and been given fresh clothing.

"Ah!" exclaimed Lord Edmund as they entered the gatehouse. "Syart, isn't it? Do you know Tamur, I almost have a certain respect for this thief, albeit on occasion he has reached the limit of my patience. Do you know that my whole army has been looking for him? Every time he manages to slip through the net, but it appears that we have him at last. So, Master Syart, we meet at last."

"Yes, my lord, but I was doing no wrong this time," whined Syart, unconvincingly.

"You never do, do you? Right, let us start from the beginning and leave nothing out, however strange."

"Well my lord," began Syart in his best speaking voice. "Me and my men were travelling, that is to say we were on the trail of something quite important, when we came across a campfire. Naturally we asked for shelter."

"Naturally" agreed Lord Edmund.

"Then it was like, like the night dropped on one of my men," continued Syart. "When we could see again, he was dead. Ripped to pieces he was. I've never seen anything like it before in my life. Horrible mutilations were on his back and his neck. I had to turn away, it was so bad. The attack was quite unprovoked and so we burned the cart in retaliation. The next thing I saw was a multitude of multi-coloured star shapes that appeared from nowhere. Then the cart which we had burned suddenly appeared without so much as a mark on it. Then, and this beats all, a great black Timber Cat, the biggest I've ever seen, comes out from the surrounding darkness. Well we tried to run but we must have blacked out, because the next thing I remember, we were all in your... er... amenities, sire."

"I believe you, Syart," said Lord Edmund, "although your explanation of the events of that evening may be somewhat distorted." He turned to the soldiers' room. "Watch Commander, keep these renegades here until their cases can be heard and befitting punishment is awarded. They already have one or two complaints to answer for and it will save time having to look for them again."

"It will be as you command, my lord."

"Do you really believe his story?" asked Lord Tamur of Lord Edmund as they walked slowly back to their offices.

"Yes, my boy, I do," replied Lord Edmund. "The events that were described are quite well-known to me, but I have to concede that nothing like this has happened for many years. The Timber Cat is a huge beast of immense power but equal tenderness. He is a companion of Birch."

"Do you mean *the* Birch? The one that you used to tell me stories about when I was a child?"

"Yes, and if our guests have managed to get mixed up with him, well they will be better off locked up, at least they will be safe. I suppose the truth of the matter will eventually surface, it usually does in time. For the moment I think that the preparations for our journey to Castle Tezz should be speeded up. Something is going on, and I for one do not like the smell of it."

"All right, father. I will attend to it straight away."

CHAPTER FOUR

Birch had been travelling a northerly route on his way to Dronecet Castle for four days. He had a feeling of frustration, because although he had been hearing magical vibrations, he could not pinpoint the source. He knew instinctively that the spells had an inclination towards a northerly direction, and that they ended at or around Dronecet Castle. However, where they originated eluded him. These events were extremely disturbing because it could only mean that somewhere, someone with the capability of using superior powers was initiating magic, and up until this point in time, and for the past fifty years, there hadn't been anyone with enhanced powers except himself.

Birch considered the possibility of it being Lord Zelfen, but he was still held powerless by the rune markings of his prison, The Watch. Master Elio, he believed, had perished when he passed on his powers over fifty years before, and that effectively ruled him out of the equation. Who could it be? The question rebounded across the temples of his mind.

He was still deep in thought when four renegades who had, in their misguided wisdom, decided to travel on the main south road, headed in his direction. They had stayed for a few days in the village of Spard, and had planned to travel across country in the hope of intercepting Aluen. They saw Birch from a distance and rode to intercept him.

"This might be Aluen of Tybow," said one of the renegades.

The four renegades, as though by silent command, dismounted and walked swiftly towards him.

"Greetings, my good man," called one of the renegades. "Would your name by any chance be Aluen of Tybow?"

"Forgive me, but I'm afraid not." Birch was wary as he continued to walk past the renegades.

"Hey! Just hold on a minute my friend."

Birch halted and slowly turned to face them.

"Are you certain that you are not Aluen of Tybow? We were told that he would be travelling this road." The renegades seemed edgy.

"Who is this Aluen of Tybow?" asked Birch, who now had some interest.

"Someone whom we have travelled a long distance

to meet," said another of the renegades, and in so doing he noticed a heavy purse attached to Birch's belt.

"Well I am sorry that I can't help you. Maybe if you enquired at Castle Tezz. It's about two days' ride from here." Birch was trying to be helpful.

"Maybe you can help." The renegade looked around, and seeing that Birch was truly alone, stepped forward to bar his way. "Maybe you can help us by handing over your purse. It looks rather heavy for such a small fellow like you."

"I don't think I would like to do that," replied Birch.

"Well maybe we will just take it anyway." The four renegades drew their swords and began hacking away at... thin air. "Where did he go?" said one. They were now confused.

"I'm here." Birch had reappeared about ten feet away from the huddled group. "Haven't you got families to go home to without causing yourselves problems?"

"We have no problems." The renegades began to advance.

"Oh but I think you have." Birch began to chant a spell of temporary change. He twisted and leapt, and a glow surrounded him.

The renegades began to laugh at what they

thought to be an amusing spectacle. "He's dancing and singing us a song, perhaps we should join in" said one. As one they suddenly charged, but something was wrong. The world, or their view of it, seemed to change. Things as they knew them were different.

Birch continued his journey, leaving four horses wondering where their masters were and four small fluffy white rabbits with an identity crisis. Although he was none too fond of using magic for the sake of it, on this occasion he felt justified, and the effects would last for only a short while. In an explosion of multi-coloured stars, he transported himself to the outskirts of Tybow and took a leisurely stroll into the village. After asking directions, one of the villagers in the square pointed him towards the local blacksmith's workshop. He could hear the sound of hammers on metal, and he could smell the forge as he approached the open doorway.

A fairly broad man, sweat dripping from his forehead, worked on a horseshoe. He eyed it for shape then dipped it in cold water. Steam fought to escape and hissed for a moment before being placed alongside three others on a bench. Wiping the sweat from his forehead with a cloth, Aluen's father noticed Birch for the first time.

"Good day to you, my friend."

"Good day to you, Blacksmith. Forgive the

intrusion upon your most valued work, but I have been led to believe that this is the residence of a Master Aluen."

"It is indeed," admitted a proud father. "But I'm afraid that he is not here at the moment."

"Oh."

"I apologise if you have come a long way to see my son, but he has gone on a journey. Can I be of assistance? I'm his father."

"Will he be back soon?" enquired Birch.

"I'm afraid that I cannot tell you when he will return. Who may I ask is inquiring after my son?"

At that point a neighbour arrived. "Good day Blacksmith," he called.

"Good day to you, neighbour. This gentleman is enquiring after Aluen, but heaven knows when he will be back."

"Thank you for your trouble, Blacksmith." Birch didn't want to take part in any conversation with the neighbourhood. He left the blacksmith to his work and the neighbour with a question forming on his lips.

"Who was that?" asked the neighbour when Birch was out of sight.

"He didn't say. I wonder why he asked for Aluen. He probably wanted to borrow one of his magic tricks or illusions."

"He ought to buy his own," said the neighbour.

Aluen, although quite oblivious to the events that surrounded him, did wonder why he was receiving all this help during his quest, especially from such an accomplished magician as Master Elio. It seemed to Aluen that Master Elio was just as impatient for him to finish the journey as he was to find out what the parchment meant. "Finish your quest" he had said, as though everything depended upon it and its outcome. Unknown to Aluen, everything did depend on it.

He followed the River Dete and then the River Powle on his way southward, and at the close of the day while he was preparing another campsite, he checked the cart because he had had little opportunity to do so earlier. He hadn't inspected it closely since it had been magically reassembled by Master Elio. The cart, after a closer inspection than would normally have been the case, appeared to be of improved quality. The joints and springs were in excellent condition, and although Aluen hated to admit it, they were better that when his father had quickly assembled them. He was very satisfied, and danced around the cart singing his praises to whoever would listen.

Something did, and Aluen was aware that he was being watched. He remembered the friendly association with the Timber Cat and knew he was safe. It was a most unusual event, and one that would take some believing. Several times during his journey he had stopped to collect firewood; there might not be any where he elected to make camp, and it would save him having to search during what would become a very cold night.

He prepared another pot of marrowbone broth to keep the warmth in and then, as the night drew to a close and black clouds covered the land, he sat by the warmth of the campfire, watched the insects flying around the oil lamps and drifted off into a dreamless sleep. In the distance two luminous eyes kept watch until daybreak.

Aluen had dreams of the parchment during the night, and when he awoke he was even more determined to discover the meaning of the words written on it. Continuing his journey, he asked several farmers if they knew of any round buildings locally, but none of them had any idea. These were recent settlers and knew little of the history of the area. It was suggested that he enquire in Forest Town. This had originally been called Hib, but expansion and public opinion had called for a new name, and as it was only two days' ride from the Forest of Frezfir, the name Forest Town was adopted. As would be expected with such a name, the main industry was timber. The town's construction was also of timber, but stone foundations protected the buildings against the possibility of flooding. The town's layout was in the form of a cross with four neat rows of buildings extending to the points of the compass.

As Aluen entered the town's perimeter on the third day of his travels, he noted how busy it appeared to be. Two men stood arguing about further development ideas as he steered his cart along one of the four outreaching streets. Faces appeared at windows as he arrived at the centre. There was a well-kept green and signposts showing the names and directions of the four streets. This was something Aluen had not seen before, and he made a mental note of how it simplified travel.

As was the custom in these new towns, several people gathered around him. Some wanted news of other settlements, while others wanted to know where to obtain certain supplies.

"Will you be taking residence?" asked one. This was not only prompted by the man's eagerness for the town to expand, but the thought of his two unwed daughters. Aluen supplied all the information he could regarding the state of affairs in the areas he knew. He passed on information that he himself had gathered on his journey so far, and not forgetting his father, he told of his father's expertise as a blacksmith, for some had enquired about metalwork for building purposes as well as tools. When all questions were exhausted, he told the townsfolk of his small skill in creating illusions and promised a demonstration later that evening.

Although it was now the onset of winter it was quite warm in the centre of this newly-developed town. It was explained to him while he refreshed himself at the local tavern that the design of the town in a cross shielded it on all sides against winter storms. Aluen agreed that the idea had merit and appeared to work well.

He was in the process of ordering more ale and asking the landlord for the recipe when there came a great shout of distress from outside. Along with the rest of the customers, he immediately went outside to find out what the trouble was. People were running in all directions and panic showed on their worried faces. Some were shouting for weapons, a cry that was taken up by some of the senior townsfolk. A young mother snatched up her child from the street and ran indoors.

"What is the matter? Why is everyone in a state of panic?" called the owner of the tavern from behind his serving table.

"Look!" one of the people pointed a bony finger.

Aluen looked in the direction indicated and

smiled. "I must apologise" he said to his fellow drinkers. There is no danger."

"What!" A worried mother, voice trembling, pointed again. "You call that no danger?"

"None at all" replied Aluen and called. "Cat!"

The huge beast turned its head and seeing Aluen, walked up to him and lay down at his feet.

"We will have to stop meeting like this." He ran his fingers through Cat's thick fur. Cat simply purred her contentment and rolled over with her paws in the air.

"See," he explained to the townsfolk, stroking Cat's underside. "Tame as a new born baby, but please be warned not to fuss her too much, and I would advise you not to make any sudden moves."

"How did you manage to tame the brute?" The question came from the owner of the tavern.

"It's a long story my friend, but I haven't trained her. No one can train a Timber Cat. She just finds me irresistible."

A peal of laughter appeared to calm the tense situation. "I wouldn't mind having her to guard my tavern. Is she for sale?"

Aluen smiled. "No I'm afraid not. You see, Cat doesn't belong to anyone. She chooses her own friends and her own company. I just happen to be the flavour of the month, so to speak."

He had no idea if that was the truth about his strange relationship with Cat, but he knew that what he said did carry some reasonable expectation. A crowd had assembled now, all of them eager to see this enormous beast while at the same time keeping their distance. Aluen stood at the centre of the crowd and was speaking to the owner of the tavern, while Cat was being Cat, sleeping with eyes only partially closed. After a while he apologised for the disturbance caused by Cat's appearance and begged the crowd to disperse. He wasn't entirely sure that Cat was enjoying all the attention and he didn't want any accidents to occur due to some over-attentive person taking liberties.

Eventually the townsfolk went back to their daily routines, while Aluen began to work out a programme for the evening's entertainment. Time seemed to pass quickly and, as the sun lowered itself onto the horizon, Aluen set lamps in a semi-circle around his cart. This was to add effect while at the same time allowing the audience to witness his demonstration, and soon a crowd of the town's folk had gathered in eager anticipation of a long-awaited distraction from the boredom of their daily routines.

Aluen began his demonstration with a selection of simple tricks. The audience applauded as he produced flowers from a cane, followed by a live rabbit from an apparently empty box. He continued by producing coloured smoke using the powders purchased from the mystic fair at Dronecet Castle. The audience was spellbound. For his finale he asked Cat to step into a large crate, which obediently she did. A beaming Aluen then made some signs with his hands for effect, and mumbled a few secret sounding words before opening the crate. Cat had disappeared. The crowd were amazed at Aluen's proficiency and even more so when, after reopening the crate, Cat had reappeared. Aluen's entertainment lasted for a full hour and the townsfolk showed their appreciation most generously. Aluen was pleased that there wasn't any fish this time, but he accepted enough meat to send back to his parents, along with an order to his father for metal brackets.

★ ★ ★

"Excuse me, Master Aluen, but I overheard a group of people talking earlier this evening. They were discussing the whereabouts of a round building in these parts, something you were perhaps looking for?"

Aluen remembered having such a conversation earlier in the tavern, but before anyone could reply to his question everyone had begun running around because Cat had appeared.

"Yes I am looking for a round building."

"Well," the man continued. "I seem to recall that there was a round building, a tower in fact. It's maybe a week to ten days' ride from here by the sea on the southern coastline."

"Thank you sir, you have been most helpful. Might I offer you something for your trouble? Please sit and share a bottle with me."

"Thank you, but no" said the ageing farmer. "I have to be up early in the morning." With that he said his goodbyes and walked away into the dark. When he had travelled a reasonable distance, he disappeared in a shower of multi-coloured stars.

Aluen danced another little jig in celebration of the news. He now thought he knew the whereabouts of the building mentioned in the parchment. It was by the sea, although the mention of a fortune there and the warning still had to be worked out; 'and mind the letters taken one by one, a fortune there to find'. He wondered if the building had protection. Maybe guards were there to protect the treasure? He would not take anything if it belonged to someone else, but then he had a thought. Why go to all the trouble of producing a parchment with details of a treasure written on it if the treasure was not to be taken? There again there might not be any treasure and this could be a fool's errand. He retired to his campsite, and after his evening meal he bedded down for the night with the promise of an early start.

Birch, still bewildered by the strange events of the past few weeks, transported himself to Dronecet Castle. He materialised just outside the sightline of the castle guards behind a small rise in the terrain. After checking himself over, he walked swiftly up to the castle. A sentry on duty called out as Birch neared the castle's main entrance.

"Hold! Who seeks entrance to Dronecet Castle?" The official-looking guard looked down from the high walls before disappearing, to reappear again by the gates.

"I have come to speak with the lord of this castle," replied Birch.

"And who shall I say requests an audience with Lord Edmund?"

"A friend." Birch was reluctant to advertise his presence.

"And does this friend have a name?" enquired the guard.

"Just say to your Lord Edmund that he gave something to me a long time ago, and I have come to thank him."

"I will do as you ask, stranger, but without a name I have little confidence that you will be granted an audience. Please wait here." The guard indicated that

Birch should wait in the guard house before he turned smartly, and in regimental fashion, marched over to the offices where Lord Edmund and Lord Tamur were still discussing the proposed journey to Castle Tezz. The guard knocked gently on the office door before entering.

"Excuse me my lords."

"Yes, what brings you away from your duties?" enquired Lord Tamur.

"There is a person at the guard house who requests an audience and wishes to speak with Lord Edmund, my lord. I have asked him for a name but with respect, my lord, all he would say is that Lord Edmund gave him something a long time ago. He further says that he has come to extend his thanks, my lord."

"What should we do, Father?" said Lord Tamur.

Lord Edmund thought for a while before giving an answer. "I am afraid that I am at a loss to think who this person is. Bring him to me under guard, we cannot be too careful. Let us see who this person is."

With your permission, my lord, I shall return shortly."

The soldier saluted, and then hurried away. He returned almost immediately with Birch under guard. Lord Edmund could hardly believe his eyes when he saw that the stranger was Birch. It had been over fifty years, but the memories were still fresh in his mind.

"All right guards, you can return to your duties. I will speak with this stranger alone."

The guards were mystified as to who the stranger was, but obeyed without question and marched away.

"You look a little older, my dear friend." Lord Edmund could hardly contain himself as he walked over to Birch and embraced him.

"Excuse me, but have I missed some vital point here?" Lord Tamur had never met Birch. To him, Birch looked like a woodsman and he failed to understand the warm welcome given by his father.

"Oh I am sorry, my son. I was lost in a time long before your birth. May I present to you Master Birch." He turned to Birch. "Master Birch, my son Lord Tamur. You will no doubt remember the name."

"Indeed I do and it will not be forgotten through your son Edmund."

"Is this *the* Master Birch?" enquired Lord Tamur, "the person you have mentioned on more than one occasion during my earlier years? I might have expected someone dressed for the part."

"Looks can be deceiving, but, yes, this is the very same Master Birch."

Lord Tamur was stunned. A man straight out of a fairy tale stood before him.

"Sir, I am at a loss for words" he said. "Greetings

to you, Master Birch. I have to admit that I would have expected someone of greater age than your good self."

"Greetings to you also, Tamur. In answer to your question, time has been good to me, and time has been good to your father too, although in a different way. He has produced a son, the image of himself as a young man. Be proud of your name also, for it holds treasured memories."

The introductions finally over, Lord Edmund led the party to the main hall, where refreshments were being served. Jaelia, Lord Edmund's wife, was introduced to Birch as she served a selection of foods. Continually busy, she supervised all the kitchen staff, but when it came to serving her husband, she alone would take care of the meals. Birch was impressed by Jaelia, and congratulated Lord Edmund on his choice of partner. When they had refreshed themselves with wine and a platter of cold meats and hot bread, Lord Edmund was the first to speak.

"It has been a long time, Master Birch. Your visit, I presume, is not an entirely social one."

"To be truthful, Edmund, I am not quite sure that coming here will help me. I have, over the last few weeks, been hearing magical vibrations from around this area. I cannot quite pinpoint the actual source of these vibrations, but I do know that they were directed towards this castle. I feel duty bound to investigate these events for obvious reasons. It might be nothing to do…"

"Good heavens," interrupted Lord Edmund who had been deep in thought. "One moment, I might be able to shed some light on these strange occurrences, Guard!"

A soldier, who had been on duty standing just outside the door, came rushing into the hall. He drew his sword in one fluid movement. "My Lords," called the soldier as he looked around to see if there were any threats towards them.

"Put away your sword," Lord Edmund smiled. "There are no enemies amongst us. Go to the guard house and escort the prisoners… no, just escort the renegade Syart to me. We would ask him some more questions."

The soldier hurried away to the guard house and informed the guard commander of Lord Edmund's request. Syart, although reluctant, was immediately escorted under guard to Lord Edmund who waited in the main hall. When they arrived, the escort was asked to wait outside, despite the protests of the guard commander, who always had the best interests of his superiors at heart. After being reassured that no harm would befall them, he reluctantly led his men into the outside passageway to await further instructions.

"Good day to you, Master Syart. I trust that you slept well and that you are being looked after with courtesy and kindness," said Lord Edmund as soon as the guards had left the hall.

"I slept like a log, my lord" replied Syart as he shifted about nervously.

"Do stop shuffling about and take a seat. Are you being well treated?"

"Very well thank you, my lord." Syart sat down. "May I be permitted to ask why I was brought here?"

"This gentleman" said Lord Edmund pointing to Birch, "has travelled some distance to ask you, if you will be so kind, to repeat the story you told me. Do not tell the entire story, just inform this gentleman of the main points."

"As is your wish, my lord". He turned to face Birch. "Well, to cut a very long story short, we, that is my friends and I, we burned a cart to keep warm. Then, and I'm not making this up, the sky was filled with multi-coloured stars. The next thing I know, the cart is back in one piece."

"How do you mean, in one piece?" asked Birch.

"It was exactly what I said, Sir. We burned it. We destroyed it so to speak. It was just ashes and bits of metal but it was there again, all put back together as good as new. There wasn't a burn mark on it. We were frightened, but when we tried to run there was a huge Timber Cat…"

"What?" interrupted Birch.

"A huge Timber Cat, Sir. It bounded out from the darkness. Honest, it was the biggest creature I'd ever seen. If I ever get my hands on that Aluen of Tybow, I'll…"

"I beg your pardon?" Lord Edmund looked startled.

"My lord?"

"What was the name you just mentioned?"

"Master Aluen of Tybow, my lord.

"That's peculiar, you didn't mention that name before when you told the story."

"I must have forgotten, my lord."

"All right, that will be all for now."

The guard commander was recalled to escort Syart back to the guard house. His relief showed as he was led out of the hall.

"Has this helped you at all, Birch?" asked Lord Edmund.

"Maybe it has. How is it that Syart is locked away in your confinement cells?"

"Master Syart, Syart the renegade, is well known to us. He is a rather elusive thief whom we have been seeking for a very long time, without much success I might add. Then the strangest course of events started. People began to appear swimming in the castle cesspit." Birch could not help but smile. "There have been eleven so far, and all have said under examination that they hadn't the slightest idea how they got there. Syart's testimony was that he began running away from a Timber Cat, the event occurring some miles away to the south east, when suddenly, and without any kind of warning, he was in our cesspit. Even I am confused."

Birch, who was deep in thought, paced the floor for quite some time deliberating on the information he had received. "Well," he said after some considerable time. "Cat is obviously part of this story. I am completely in the dark as to who the magician is, but he must be friendly because Cat is with him. She wouldn't stay with anyone without good reason. Master Aluen's name has cropped up before, but I can't remember his name being associated with anything to do with the arts. He appears to be a central character in these events and I would very much like to meet him, but first I think I will pay another visit to Castle Tezz. I also think that under the circumstances, we should be on our guard. It may be unnecessary but there again it may be dangerous."

"Well we are preparing to journey to Castle Tezz for much the same reason as you," announced Lord Edmund. "It would give us great pleasure if you would accompany us."

"It would be my pleasure and I would be delighted."

And so it was, that on a cold and frosty morning, a small group escorted by twelve men-at-arms from an elite defence group left Dronecet Castle en route to Castle Tezz. The soldiers remaining at the castle were ordered to stay on alert for anything out of the ordinary happening in the area.

CHAPTER FIVE

Time, a war which no single man can ever win, no nation in its entirety can defeat; the ticking of that eternal clock which stops for no man. The everlasting pendulum of passing days, where one swing could make the difference between light and dark, between summer and winter, between success or failure. A millionth part of a second that could determine between war and peace, between life... and death.

Aluen, during the remaining journey to what he believed to be his destination, decided to stay in the village of Goston for a day. It was good to have a break and it provided the opportunity to give a demonstration of his competence in performing tricks and illusions once again. The pleasure and appreciation of the villagers was shown in the usual fashion, and Aluen again sent produce home to his parents.

After a good night's rest and twelve days of travel, Aluen finally neared his destination. He was pleased with the time he had spent travelling and the people he had met, but now, wrapped up warmly as a protection against the cold sea wind, Aluen stood motionless, his eyes feasting on the vision before him. Standing no more than two hundred yards away, and perched on the edge of a steep cliff, was the tall, round building which he hoped was the one mentioned in the parchment. He reflected again at the time it had taken him to reach this point.

The grey stone structure stood like an ancient monument, and was covered with an invading blanket of green algae. It had stood the force of nature and the sea. Drum beats echoed the mighty strength of the ocean, cymbals clashed as waves constantly beat their anger against the rocks and walls of the building. White spray permeated the air and Aluen began to get quite wet. Occasionally, the melancholy scream of a sea bird added to the thunderous noise, a cry in the wilderness as it rested, wings spread on the buffeting wind currents. Clouds hung heavy in the sky like unwashed blankets, and there was a greyness that was quite unnerving.

Aluen was apprehensive as he approached the building. Was this really the building mentioned in the parchment? Had he been on a fool's errand? He was almost afraid to find out. This must be his goal, he thought. With a kind of reverence he moved forward, but almost stumbled as sea spray whipped up by the mighty waves descended like fine rain to make the stony ground slippery underfoot. He wiped his face with the sleeve of his tunic as he approached the entrance to the building, a thick wooden door bound with rusted metal straps. He turned the large metal handle, and, surprisingly, the door swung open on well-greased metal hinges. He nervously stepped inside.

"Hello!" he called, but there was no answer. The room was very dry and compared with the outside temperature, it was also very warm. This seemed strange considering the location and the fact that there were no fires in evidence.

Noticing that the room was quite large and had stone steps leading upwards in a spiral, he removed his cloak and laid it on the steps after shaking off the globules of sea spray, and then he began to investigate. Initially he could see nothing of great value; no chests overflowed with gold and there were no bags containing precious jewels. As his eyes became accustomed to the dim light provided by torches mounted on the walls, he noticed that there were strange symbols on these walls. Closer examination revealed them to be made from precious metals, and although blackened with age, each individual symbol was worth a considerable amount.

Was this then the treasure?

He decided to investigate this strange building further. He began to climb the stone staircase, and as he did so, he discovered that all the walls of the building were covered with these strange but precious symbols, and at the top of the multitude of stone steps a single door was likewise covered with the unusual markings.

"Hello?" called a voice.

Aluen was shaken and almost ran back down the spiral staircase.

"Congratulations!" called the voice.

Aluen peered through a grille which was set centrally in the wooden door, and which allowed viewing into the room beyond. On a single chair, a figure sat, smiling.

"Come in dear boy, come in" called the occupant of the room.

Aluen slowly opened the door. He failed to notice that for some reason there were no handles on the inside of the door with which to open it. Had he done so, he might have been a little more cautious.

"Good day to you, sir," said Aluen.

"Good day to you, young man. At long last someone has won." A smiling Lord Zelfen took hold of Aluen's hand and shook it vigorously, while at the same time he held the door open with his foot.

"Won?" Aluen was puzzled.

"Yes, won, my dear, dear boy. Some years ago I decided to give away my fortune. I planned to seek a solitary life based on prayer and meditation. To this end I devised a riddle that only intelligent people would understand, and I vowed that I would stay here until it was solved," lied Lord Zelfen.

"You did?"

"Yes and today young man, I apologise but you didn't give me your name."

"Aluen of Tybow, sir."

"Of course, today, Master Aluen of Tybow, you have earned this reward. Did you notice all the symbols that I have had placed around the walls of this building to bring me good fortune?"

"Yes."

"They are made from the finest quality silver, a very precious metal. Today, Master Aluen of Tybow, they are yours for the taking as a reward for solving my riddle. I will spend the rest of my days in the poverty of my chosen religion."

"Thank you so much, sir."

"Go on and help yourself. Take them all." Lord Zelfen was still holding the door open with a well-placed foot.

Aluen was at a loss. He didn't know where to start, but he soon began collecting the silver symbols. His cart was a short distance away, so he began to pile up the symbols at the bottom of the spiral staircase. Lord Zelfen watched with keen interest as the runes were taken one by one, knowing that with each one he was taking a further step towards freedom. He was determined that no one would have the opportunity to imprison him again, and certainly not in this place.

For what seemed to be an age, Aluen worked methodically in the collection all of the symbols. He was feverish with happiness and excitement. This amount of silver would mean financial security, not only for himself, but for his parents, for the remainder of their lives.

Eventually the last of the symbols was removed, and Lord Zelfen, congratulating Aluen once again by wishing him a prosperous future, felt freedom for the first time in over fifty years; the freedom he had yearned.

Aluen was busy loading his cart with the silver when Lord Zelfen approached him again.

"I have just one tiny request if I might be so bold as to ask, Master Aluen of Tybow."

"I will fulfil any request, anything that I am able to do, sir."

"Good. When you leave here I would ask that you deliver a message to Castle Tezz. I would like you to say to Lord Torran that Lord Zelfen sends his greetings and…"

"Lord Zelfen? Oh I am sorry, my lord. I was not aware of your nobility." Aluen knelt before him.

"Get yourself up Master Aluen. You have no idea how much you have helped me by solving the riddle of the parchment."

"Thank you my lord."

"All right, now where was I? Oh yes, tell Lord Torran that we will be meeting in the fullness of time. He will understand."

"I will deliver your message with the utmost urgency, my lord."

Lord Zelfen mumbled a few words and sent a spell of pain to Birch. "That will do for a start", he said to himself, and then to Aluen he said, "I see by the look of the boxes on your cart that you perform illusions."

"I try, my lord."

"Well I bet you can't do this one." At this he disappeared.

★ ★ ★

Lord Edmund's group transport consisted of two covered wagons. A bodyguard of twelve mounted guardsmen, along with spare horses, had travelled alongside, and with the exception of periods of darkness, had journeyed non-stop for eight days. On the sixth day they had passed through the village of

Tybow where Aluen's parents, along with other villagers, had stood and waved their respect to the lord's colours. After crossing the River Powle on the ninth day, a sudden, unexpected and mysterious illness had gripped Birch. He had fallen and was doubled up with excruciatingly severe pains. Lord Tamur immediately halted the journey and organised an encampment with the guards taking defensive positions.

"What ails you, Birch?" he enquired.

Birch had no explanation. It was the first time in his life that such a pain had taken his strength. Then, as quickly as the pain had gripped him and ripped through his body, it disappeared with no trace of its origin and no after effects.

The pains came again later that day and Birch was advised to travel in the back of one of the wagons. A messenger was dispatched to inform the Border House Commander of the group's impending arrival, and that one of their company had taken ill. The pain again lasted but for a short while, and the rest of that day was spent in comparative comfort. However, Jaelia, Lord Edmund's wife, would not hear of Birch walking or riding. She ordered him to stay resting. Lord Edmund explained that Jaelia was extremely strong-willed, and it would be pointless to argue with her. He had tried on several occasions, but had had to give in finally. Birch took the hint and was well advised to do so because, on the tenth day, the pain returned with a vengeance. It was as though his insides were being trampled on, twisted and pulled. On one occasion he lost consciousness and Lord Edmund began to have grave concerns for his friend.

As they continued their journey with Jaelia tending Birch, the group came upon a figure standing in the middle of the road. They came to a halt and the guards immediately surrounded the wagon. The figure was dressed in black robes, and a hood not only covered his head but hid his face from view. In his hand he held a large, unusually carved staff.

"I can cure his illness," called the figure in a low, but melodic voice.

"How do you come to know that we have a sick person with us?" called Lord Tamur who sat on the lead wagon. He was puzzled by this person.

"I know many things," replied the figure as he approached Lord Tamur's wagon. "Show me where he lies."

For no apparent reason, Lord Edmund felt at ease with this stranger and climbed down from his seat. "Come," he said, and directed the hooded stranger to the rear of the wagon. "He lies in the back. But be warned, if any further harm comes to my friend there will be consequences."

The hooded figure, his face still covered, climbed into the wagon. He rested his staff on Birch and began to chant. A spark that went unnoticed by Lord Edmund and Jaelia appeared to leap from the staff and on to Birch.

"He will sleep now and he will be refreshed when he awakes," explained the mysterious stranger.

"Will he suffer any further pains?" asked Jaelia.

"No, the pains are no more."

Both Lord Edmund and his wife were confused by the stranger's actions. He had not examined Birch, yet he maintained that the illness would trouble him no further. They climbed out of the wagon and Lord Edmund looked back at the now sleeping Birch, but when he turned again to thank the stranger for his efforts, he had disappeared; he was nowhere to be seen. This confused him and the incident remained in his mind for the remainder of the day.

As the group halted and began to make camp for the night, Birch's eyes flickered open. He felt refreshed and there was no sign of the agonising pain that had attacked him earlier. Rising from his bed he dressed, then climbed down from the wagon and joined the others who sat around the camp fire. Jaelia gave him a sideways look, but he reassured her that he was fine and felt better. Lord Edmund told him about the strange events that had occurred earlier in the day, but no-one, and this included Birch, could throw any light on who the stranger might have been.

"We never saw his face," explained Lord Tamur.

As was promised the pains did not return, and after twelve days of travel the group reached the Border House. This was a welcomed chance to refresh themselves before starting on the last leg of their journey to Castle Tezz.

Not far from Forest Town at a place where Birch had met the four unfortunate renegades, the same four reappeared by the roadside. One was still busy eating grass.

"What happened? Where did that traveller go?" asked one of the renegades.

"How should I know?" replied another as he spat out the grass and wondered why he was eating it in the first place.

The other two renegades were still trying to hop around and resembled kangaroos, until they faced each other. They immediately stopped and felt quite embarrassed. Their horses, fortunately for them, were still grazing at the side of the road.

"Come on you lot, we have to intercept Master Aluen, otherwise Syart will be angry with us. We can get some money from the next traveller we meet," said the leader of the group.

The four renegades mounted their horses and set

off at a slow pace. For almost six days they had travelled southward, and as they neared Forest Town they spied another traveller. He was alone and was wearing fine black robes with a hood that covered his face. It appeared that he was coming from Forest Town and the renegades thought he might be a merchant of some sort.

"This one is mine," announced one of the band. He halted his horse a few yards from the traveller.

"Good day to you, Merchant" began the renegade. "I, er, my friends and I were wondering if by any chance we could relieve you of your purse, and your fine robes. They do look a little shabby on you, but they will probably fit me perfectly." He laughed. The stranger was without movement.

"You see," continued the renegade, "we have had a little bad luck recently, and you could be the answer to all of our problems, including the financial ones."

"Well, this is just not your day, is it?" remarked the strangely-robed figure. At that the renegades disappeared. The strangely-robed figure carried on walking, the four horses following him. Under his hood the figure was giggling to himself and thinking of the renegades' arrival at Dronecet Castle. Cat was not far behind.

"Excuse me, my lord." The guard saluted Lord Torran.

"What is it?"

"My Lord, there is a person at the guard house. He says that his name is Master Aluen of Tybow and he requests an audience. He also appears to be quite wealthy, my lord. His cart overflows with silver of the highest quality."

"Direct him to the main hall, I will see him there."

"As you command my lord." The soldier marched smartly away.

Aluen was pacing the guard house a little impatiently because, having found the treasure he was looking for, he wanted to return home. He had not seen his parents for some time and was eager to share his good fortune with them. He was examining some old weaponry on the walls when the soldier returned, and he was escorted through the castle grounds to the main hall. Lord Torran was standing by a large open fire when Aluen was escorted into the hall. The soldier, mindful of his duties, stood at the door in case he was needed further.

"Lord Torran?" asked Aluen with a graceful bow.

"Indeed it is, Master Aluen. How can I help you?"

"Well, my lord" said Aluen. "I am not in need of any help. I have come to deliver a message."

"And what is this message?"

"The message is, my lord..." Aluen tried to remember the exact words. "That Lord Zelfen sends his greetings, and says that you and he will be meeting in the fullness of time. That is the message, my lord."

"You have spoken with Lord Zelfen? When, how and where did you meet him?" Lord Torran was clearly agitated.

"Yes my lord, I have spoken to him, it's how I received the message. It was less than a week ago when we met. You see, I found a kind of map on a parchment at a mystic fair that was held at Dronecet Castle. The map showed promise of a fortune in treasure if the riddle contained within the map could be solved. Well, I solved it. The clues led me to a huge round building by the south coast, and that's where I met Lord Zelfen. He said that because I had solved the riddle, I could have all the silver lettering and symbols that adorned the walls of the building. He was such a nice gentleman, and the promise that he would devote the remainder of his life to prayer and meditation is worthy of respect, my lord."

Lord Torran almost burst out laughing, but was too devastated to do so. "Did you say that you removed all of the letters and symbols from the building?"

"Yes my lord. Lord Zelfen was insistent that I take every one."

"Oh no, please wait here for a moment. I have to inform some people of these developments." Lord

Torran walked to the door, and then ran as fast as he could push doors open as he went until he reached Lord Karl's offices. "Karl! He shouted."

I'm here, my pug-nosed friend" called Lord Karl.

"No time for games, ratface. Lord Zelfen has escaped."

"Do you mean to tell me that he is no longer a prisoner in the Watch?" replied a concerned Lord Karl.

"I mean exactly that."

Lord Karl opened a window and shouted at the top of his voice. "Call out the guards!" He turned back to face Lord Torran. "How do you know that he has escaped?"

"A young man by the name of Aluen of Tybow was duped by a promise of a fortune. He came to me to deliver a message and is waiting in the main hall."

"What was the message?"

"He says that Lord Zelfen sends his greetings and will meet with me in the fullness of time. He duped the young man and tricked him into taking all the letters and symbols from the walls of the Watch. Good heavens, if he comes here we will be defenceless against such an opponent!"

Master Errol and Master Terance, on hearing the shouts of orders and seeing soldiers running in all directions, went to Lord Karl's office to find out what was happening.

"Are we expecting important visitors, Father?" asked Master Terance excitedly.

Lord Torran took the two young men to one side. "Look, we have a very grave problem, and it is one that will take more than a little sorting out. It is important, therefore, that if we ask you to do something, you obey immediately and without question whatever the command. Is that understood? It could mean the difference between life and death."

"Is it that serious?" asked Master Errol.

"I'm afraid it is, so no more questions at this time. I would like you both to go to your quarters. Soldiers will shortly be at your side, and it will be their task to protect you, should protection be needed. Go now and be safe."

The seriousness of Lord Torran's words was well heeded and the two young Masters left for their respective rooms. Elanor also understood that something was wrong, but she knew her place. She was kept busy organising the castle staff, and did not interfere with matters of a military nature. She made sure that Master Errol and Master Terance were comfortable before returning to her duties. The castle guards were lined up in three ranks on the parade ground when Lord Karl, followed by Lord Torran, walked outside.

"Captain of the Guard!" called Lord Karl.

"We are at your service, my lord."

"Captain, we are facing a very serious situation, the first of its kind in a very long time. It could mean that we will have to defend ourselves against unknown enemies. At the worst we could be at war, even with our neighbours."

"We will do our duty, my lord" replied the Captain of the Guard.

"Well spoken, Captain. From this moment and until further orders are received, the castle will be on full alert. This is not an exercise. You will detail the appropriate number of guards for protection duties and they will be responsible for the safety of the ladies and the young Masters Errol and Terance. Weapon drills will increase, as will patrols. Guard duties will be doubled, as will look-outs. I will need a report if anything odd or unusual occurs within the castle grounds or within our boundaries, however slight, and I shall expect any and all reports to be handed to Lord Torran or myself immediately they occur. Is that understood?"

"Yes, my lord."

"I will need a fast horse with a trusted rider to take a message to the Border House. This will inform the Watch Commander of the situation so that he can take the appropriate steps. The message will be that Lord Zelfen has escaped, and the Border House will remain on full alert until such time that orders are received to stand down."

"I will attend to it immediately, my lord."

Within thirty minutes of the order being given, a rider on a strong horse had galloped out of the main gates en route to the Border House. The gates were then closed with a decisive thud as the two great doors came together. As the two soldiers who had closed the gates were about to return to the guard house, they noticed a dark hooded figure standing before them. Beside the figure sat a huge Timber Cat, and behind him stood four horses. The soldiers, unable to speak, backed up to the main gates. They were afraid of the sight and hoped it was an illusion.

"Have no fear, my friends. Go about your duties," said the stranger in a low, melodic voice. "Perhaps you will be so kind as to take care of the horses?"

"Of course," replied a soldier, as the burden of fear began to evaporate. "But who are you stranger, and more importantly, how did you manage to enter the castle grounds without being seen? We will have to report this, you know."

"All doors are open to me, young man. Go quickly and tell Lord Torran and Lord Karl that I am here."

The soldiers, still very nervous due to recent orders, were only too pleased to be given the chance to get away. One of the soldiers, after a little argument, ran off towards the main hall while the other, wondering who it was that commanded such attention, led the horses to the stables. Aluen, who at the time had returned to the gate house to await Lord Torran's pleasure, wandered outside for some air. He immediately noticed Cat, ran over to her and hugged her around her vast neck. Cat responded by washing Aluen's face with long drawn-out strokes of a wide, pink tongue.

"Good day, Master Aluen of Tybow," said the hooded stranger.

Aluen looked up, but could not see the man's face. Then, after a few seconds, realisation dawned. "Master Elio!" he exclaimed in surprise.

"I am the very same, young Master Aluen. But wait, for your questions will be answered. All will become clear in due course."

"How did you know I was going to ask a question?"

"There you go, you have just asked one."

Aluen laughed as he continued to stroke Cat. A moment later, Lord Torran and Lord Karl arrived at the gate.

"Master Aluen, are you safe with that creature?" asked a concerned Lord Karl.

"He's as gentle as a newborn kitten, aren't you Cat?"

Cat purred in answer, and it sounded like a miniature drum roll.

"Just a minute," Lord Torran's mind recalled scenes from half a lifetime ago. "This cannot be Cat, Master Birch's Cat. Master Birch has gone to the North in search of her."

"I don't think she belongs to anyone," said Aluen. "All I can say is that we get along quite well. Who is Master Birch anyway?"

"Oh, never mind," replied Lord Karl. "Who is your companion?" He indicated the hooded figure.

"Do you not know me, Lord Karl of Wind and Water? Torran of Ice and Fire, have you forgotten me after only fifty years, when we have known each other for ten times that length of time?" The figure pulled the hood clear from his head and face and walked, arms outstretched, towards Lord Torran.

There was a moment of recognition as the years melted away and Lord Torran fell into the arms of his friend. Lord Karl joined in the embrace as tears of joy began to flow. "Master Elio!" he said. "We thought you had perished."

"If I remember correctly, you both thought I had perished once before. You should know by now, Torran, that I am, and always will be Master Elio. But look at you! I must say in all truthfulness that age suits you. Come, let us adjourn to the main hall, I feel a feast coming on."

The friends and Cat made their way to the main hall where food was usually prepared and stories were exchanged of the old times. Master Aluen could do little but gaze starry-eyed at the three men as they repeated the tales of the Lords of Magic. He heard of the battles with the elements, and of Birch, the Master of all magic. Masters Errol and Terance were also allowed to join in the celebrations, and were introduced to Master Elio, who, after holding their hands for a long time, blessed them both with health and happiness and promised to leave them each a gift before he departed the land once more.

"If I were but a thousand years younger!" proclaimed Master Elio when he was introduced to Elanor, Lord Torran's wife. She blushed and made her excuses that work could not stop and tasks could not be completed by themselves. She left the men to their conversations.

"Does Master Birch truly exist then?" asked Aluen.

"For the moment he does, young Master Aluen of Tybow, but times are changing. The world is changing and we are changing. There is no longer a place for magical beings, because magic can be misused. In time, all that we are will be forgotten. For now, my young friend, we have work to do. You have completed the task set for you, which was to release Lord Zelfen so that he might participate in the final battle. I know that all might seem like a game to you, but it is much more than that because if the battle is won, and I have no hand in the outcome, then the world as you know it will be free to live in the light. Your task now, Master Aluen of Tybow, is to look after and care for Cat. She will begin to age after we are gone, and if one day she leaves you without explanation, she will have come to join Birch and me once again. This is why you were chosen, Aluen. You have no fear, and where others would hunt Cat, you have a love for all things, and are filled with compassion and understanding."

"But what if the final battle is lost?" asked Aluen.

"Then Cat will need you more than ever, because the world will be doomed to eternal darkness."

"How can we fight Lord Zelfen?" enquired Lord Karl.

"You can't even if you wanted to. Even before, when you were bestowed with the magic of the elements, you could not have challenged Lord Zelfen's awesome powers. Master Birch is the only one who can fight Lord Zelfen with any chance of success. They have equal abilities, more or less. Let us hope that when the time comes, Master Birch will be victorious. But come, let us not dwell on what the future might bring. Lift your goblets and let us for the moment enjoy ourselves." He raised his arms and suddenly, in a blaze of multi-coloured stars, the tables appeared dressed and filled with all manner of succulent foods. "Is anyone hungry?"

"Ah! So that's how you did it," mused Aluen.

CHAPTER SIX

Lord Edmund's party of travellers, having refreshed themselves at the Border House, were well content as they made camp atop a small rise with about two days' journey to go before reaching Castle Tezz. The night sky, which was totally clear of cloud and supported a bright full moon, was extremely cold, but the large camp fire gave out a welcoming heat and sent up tiny sparks to illuminate the darkness. Apart from the crackling of the wood, it was an unusually silent night. The countryside which was normally a hive of activity, even in winter, appeared to be holding its breath.

Lord Edmund's party had noticed a rider earlier in the day heading rapidly towards the Border House and periodically breaking the early evening's silence; this fact had given rise to speculative comment around the camp fire.

Birch was now free from the pains of a few days

ago, but he knew instinctively that something was not quite right with the land. He had no explanation for this feeling, but deep down inside he knew that something was wrong. He slept little that night, his eyes half open like a Timber Cat, as he contemplated the possibilities.

The next day Lord Edmund commented on how tired he looked. Birch dismissed the comment, saying he was restless; he didn't say why. The nagging doubt that all was not well continued for the next two days, and when the walls of Castle Tezz came into view, Birch breathed a sigh of relief because it appeared that everything was normal after all. However, there was one exception; the gates were closed, an unusual sight during the hours of daylight.

As they neared the castle gates the banners of Dronecet Castle were raised to show identification. The castle guards immediately recognised the colours as they came into view.

"Open the gates. Call out the guard!" shouted one of the guards.

"Who approaches?" called the Guard Commander.

"Lord Edmund's colours on the main road, sir," was the reply.

The soldiers were instructed to open the gates while an honour guard hurriedly dressed for the occasion formed three ranks on the parade ground. As the wagons of Lord Edmund's party entered the main gates of Castle Tezz, a fanfare was sounded in salute to his colours and to herald the arrival of important visitors. The wagons came to a halt, and after thanking the Guard Commander and passing compliments on the turnout of a well-rehearsed guard of honour, the Lords Edmund and Tamur, along with Edmund's wife Jaelia, walked slowly towards the main hall. Birch followed shortly afterwards, and when he arrived, a smile lit up his smooth face for the first time in weeks. Cat, who was lying by the fire, looked up when Birch entered the hall and padded across the stone paved floor to welcome him. He was busy fussing Cat when a voice echoed across the silence of the hall.

"Good day to you, Master Birch."

Birch stopped stroking Cat and looked up. The scene didn't register immediately, but when he realised he was looking at Master Elio standing between Lord Torran and Lord Karl, he ran across the hall to where they stood and threw himself into Master Elio's open arms. No words were necessary as tears of happiness rolled freely down his cheeks.

That evening, after everyone had refreshed themselves with a hot bath and a change of clothing, they assembled again in the main hall. Master Aluen sat with Cat by the huge log fire, while the others discussed the situation and what could be done about it. Jaelia had left the menfolk to their business and had gone to visit Lady Elanor, Lord Torran's wife. Terance and Errol stood in awe as once again they were allowed to join the company of the two masters of magic, and like the last time, Master Elio seemed to stare at the two young lords. It was as though he was looking into some future time, or a time long past.

He was awakened from his trance-like state as Lord Torran fully explained the situation and called for silence.

"We cannot stand by and give Lord Zelfen the time to raise an army. We must prevent this at all costs" He told them.

"I am of the opinion that everything will be all right, at least for the time being," said Lord Karl. "It would prove difficult to raise an army during the winter, so I believe little will happen until the summer comes, or at least until there is warmer weather."

"But you must also understand," began Master Elio in reply, "that we are not dealing with any ordinary set of circumstances. Lord Zelfen could, if he wanted, raise the dead during winter. An army of the living would therefore be of little or no difficulty by comparison."

"Master Elio is right," agreed Birch. "I must travel

in search of Lord Zelfen without delay. The gods only know what he will get up to if left to his own devices. However, it might slow him down if he knows I am following him, and he will be more cautious."

"Might I make a suggestion?" enquired Lord Tamur.

"All ideas are welcome," said Lord Karl.

"Well then, what if Master Birch could travel incognito, so to speak?"

"Go on," urged Birch.

"Well, if Master Birch were to travel along with Master Aluen, and to help him prevent being detected by Lord Zelfen he travels within Cat, the shield might make it very difficult for him to be located. They could travel all over the land without the least suspicion, and no recognition. Then when Lord Zelfen is eventually found, Master Birch would have the advantage in any planned confrontation. Surprise is always a good method of attack. We could send out groups of soldiers to rectify anything that Lord Zelfen has upset. He would expect soldiers to be sent out in any case, but a travelling illusionist, especially one who has just earned a fortune..." Lord Tamur trailed off.

Lord Torran was the first to speak. "What do you think, Master Elio?"

"Well, if Lord Zelfen suspects that he is being

followed, he could and probably would create all manner of problems for us. The way Lord Tamur suggests has merit and may give us the advantage, but I will insist upon going with them, just in case, as an observer."

"Do I have a say in this?" asked Master Aluen as he got up from near the fire to join in the group discussion.

"No!" said Master Elio and everyone laughed. "Of course you do" he continued. "It might be dangerous, but Cat will be with you, and she is very good at sorting out troublemakers."

Aluen resigned himself to the fact that he would be going on another adventure and offered no further objection to the plan. He began to look forward to travelling in the company of two of the land's most powerful men. Not only was this an honour, but a once-in-a-lifetime experience. He did mention his concern that Cat might be hurt, but Master Elio reminded him that Cat had nine lives and she hadn't used up the first one yet. Aluen just smiled.

Lord Torran suggested that the castle provide him with a much larger wagon, one with a canvas roof for shelter. "Lord Zelfen would have expected you to have purchased another more accommodating vehicle, and I believe we can supply you with four extra horses to complement the illusion" he said.

Masters Errol and Terance, who had been quiet during the conversations, asked if they too could join Aluen on his journey. Lord Karl dismissed the idea as being too dangerous for them and said they should stay in the castle where it was safer. "This is a very serious matter. It is not a game," he told them.

Although realising the seriousness of the proposed journey, Aluen was also excited. He recalled that he had solved a puzzle and been rewarded with a fortune in silver. He had met two of the most exciting wizards in the land, and he had been given a new covered wagon and four horses. Someone must be watching over him, he thought. He did feel a little remorse for his part in bringing trouble to the land, but this was unavoidable; it was meant to be and there was little he could do to prevent it.

To complete the proposed deception, for the next two hours, Aluen described his illusion boxes and how the illusions worked. To act as travelling magicians, everyone had to know how to perform in front of an audience. Master Elio was amused and offered some small feats of real magic which could be shielded from Lord Zelfen's senses, and it wasn't very long before they had the beginnings of a quite spectacular demonstration.

The morning came almost too quickly, and although it was not as cold as previous winter mornings, flakes of snow filled the air. Lord Edmund fancied that it would be in their best interests to return to Dronecet Castle before the heavy snows of winter set in. He instructed his guard to give protection to Master Elio and company for part of their journey, and so, as the huge gates of Castle Tezz were opened, Master Elio embraced Lord Torran and Lord Karl.

"I will forever be with you, my friends," he told them. Then, after climbing into the wagon and with a wave of his hand, the wagons inched forward on the next stage of their journey. They kept to the main roads for the most part, and crossed the River Powle at Spard some eight days later. It was now bitterly cold and Aluen's return journey was uneventful except for the fact that the first snows fell late one evening.

As people slept and dreamed their individual dreams, the land slowly changed colour. The browns and greens of late autumn became the blanket of whiteness that was winter. Only the evergreens defied nature, but even these had a coating of cold whiteness. Red holly berries stood out in sharp contrast against the winter blanket, and served as food for the many birds and animals that had not migrated. As morning dawned, it was noticed by everyone that the land had undergone a complete metamorphosis during the night. People awoke to a glistening white countryside, and children, well wrapped up against the cold, ran out to play their winter games in the snow.

Aluen had decided to invite Master Elio and Master Birch to the Village of Tybow for the winter, and during this four-day journey Cat had travelled in the rear of the wagon and out of sight. This was to lessen the prospect of Lord Zelfen finding out what it was that they were planning. It was decided not to perform any demonstrations during this period because it would appear out of the ordinary during the cold spell, and unless a demonstration was booked by a private party, it might attract the wrong sort of attention.

It had taken almost two weeks to travel to the Village of Tybow. As the wagon came to a halt by the blacksmith's forge, Aluen's father, who was still hard at work, came out to greet him.

"Aluen, my son!" he called with a huge smile on his face.

"Father!" Aluen jumped down from the wagon and embraced his father. "I have so much to tell you about my journey."

"I see that you have travelling companions," remarked his father, who had noticed Master Elio and Master Birch sitting on the wagon. "And a much larger wagon and four horses." He failed to notice Cat, who was still lying on the silver in the back of the wagon. "Come, all of you. Let us go inside where it is warm."

"We have something to discuss, Father, and it must be in private," announced Aluen.

"Well we have no visitors today, due to the snow I suppose."

Master Elio and Master Birch climbed down from the wagon and were escorted into the house. Although it appeared small from the outside, the inside was extremely roomy and well decorated. A table and benches occupied the main living room, and a kitchen led to the rear of the property. Behind the house was a long stretch of enclosed land which served as an area for carts, with storage space and racks for different metals. Although the main room was kept warm by an open log fire, there was a door which led to the forge, and when this was opened, more hot air was circulated during the winter periods. It also helped to heat the upper part of the house, which boasted four large sleeping rooms, two of which were directly above the workshop.

Master Elio and Master Birch were both offered seats while Aluen's mother, after greeting her son and thanking him for the provisions he had sent during his travels, served refreshments of hot spiced wine.

When all were assembled, Aluen stood up and called for silence.

"Father, Mother," he began. "I have to beg you to keep in confidence what I am about to say."

"Go on then, Aluen," encouraged his father.

"Well first of all I would like to introduce to you my travelling companions. Father, Mother, may I present to you Master Elio and Master Birch. They would, with your permission, like to stay here for the winter period."

On hearing the names of their guests, Aluen's parents fell to their knees. "My dear sirs," began Aluen's father. "We are most honoured that you should consider our humble home fit for your needs. We are simple folk, but you are both welcome to stay for as long as you deem it necessary."

Master Elio raised his hand in a friendly gesture. "Please, please rise. There is no need for you to kneel in our presence. It is we who should be kneeling at your feet. You have raised a fine boy and one with whom we have both been pleased to travel. We should therefore be very happy if you would treat us as friends. We do not seek recognition, for our journey depends upon secrecy."

"I fear that our neighbour will know you," remarked Aluen's father.

"Well we will have to help him to forget, won't we." Master Elio gave Aluen a crafty grin.

"Father, I also have a sort of permanent companion." Aluen looked over to Master Birch, hopefully.

"Yes Master Aluen of Tybow, he will be permanent, if of course you will accept this responsibility."

"Oh I will, Master Birch, I will."

"And where is this other companion? Shouldn't you have invited him inside as well?" asked Aluen's father.

"She, Father, is guarding my treasure. Come, and please do not be alarmed."

Aluen's father was puzzled by this last comment as they neared the front of the house.

"Cat!" called Aluen as he opened the door. The covered wagon rocked from side to side as Cat jumped out and came to stand by Aluen.

"Good heavens!" gasped Aluen's father. Not being the nervous type, he rubbed his hand through Cat's thick fur. "So this is the famous Timber Cat. Isn't she gorgeous?"

"Yes Father she is. Now for another surprise. Look at our four new horses which are pulling the wagon. Now wait until you see what's inside."

Aluen's father hugged his son proudly. He had shown that he had developed into manhood, and had been able to survive where others might have failed.

Aluen pulled back the cover of the wagon, and when his father saw the treasure, he was speechless. The great mountain of silver glistened where Cat's fur had polished it. "We had better bring the wagon to the back" he said.

Aluen led the horses and steered the wagon into the enclosure at the rear of the house, then, with the help of his father, he unhitched the horses and rubbed them down. "Cat will guard it for us now, Father" he said.

They both went back inside the house where, for the next hour, Aluen's father sang his son's praise. He told his wife about Cat, the wagon, the horses and the treasure.

"I chose well, I think," said Master Elio. "Now, is anyone hungry?"

"Oh no!" laughed Aluen as he caught a glimpse of the next-door neighbour through the window. "It's the gentleman from next door come to pay us a visit."

There was a polite knock on the front door. Master Elio made some strange signs with his fingers. No one noticed. The neighbour was let into the house, and after being introduced to Master Elio and Master Birch, he quite forgot who they were. He also forgot what he had come for, and left after wishing everyone a pleasant evening.

"You must be hungry," said Aluen's mother.

"I am rather peckish, as it happens." Master Elio smiled. "Allow me." He appeared to lapse into a semi-conscious state. Then, as Aluen and his parents looked on in astonishment, multi-coloured stars appeared above the table. When the stars disappeared with an audible popping sound, the table was covered with plates of food. There was steaming hot fowl, beef, mutton and a whole host of fruits and nuts. There were flasks of wine, bread and a selection of fine cheeses.

Master Birch also made a sign with his fingers and a trifle appeared, complete with a cherry on top. "Well I have to contribute as well," he laughed.

"Let's eat," suggested Aluen's father.

CHAPTER SEVEN

There was a strange atmosphere as Lord Edmund's party approached Dronecet Castle, and the guards seemed nervous, as did the rest of the small company.

"Something is not quite right here," Lord Edmund confided in the senior guardsman. "The flag isn't flying and the gates are open. I can see that there aren't any lookouts. And it's too silent." He called for Lord Tamur to join him.

"What is it, Father?"

"Tamur, I want you to wait here with two guards. Take the spare horses, and if all is well I'll call you to follow. If you don't hear anything from me within the next thirty minutes, go directly to Master Elio. He will be in the village of Tybow, and make haste. He will know what to do."

"Yes Father."

"Please be careful my son" were Lord Edmund's final words as he signalled to the remainder of the guards to carry on to the castle.

There was an eerie feeling as they passed through the castle gates. The guards were absent from their posts and the castle appeared to be deserted. They came to a halt on the parade ground, but before they could evaluate the situation, the castle gates closed with a thud as the two great doors came together.

"To me," called Lord Edmund and the ten remaining guards surrounded the wagon as Lord Edmund climbed down. Syart walked lazily from the gate house. He absent-mindedly kicked a stone as he approached Lord Edmund.

"Good day to you, my lord," he sneered.

"Good day to you, Master Syart. What may I ask is the meaning of this cold reception? Where are the guards?"

"The guards? They are all out looking for you of course. They believe that you are stuck somewhere in this not-too-clement weather. They think you are caught in a snowdrift, or something of that description."

"What, all two hundred of them?"

"There is safety in numbers my lord."

There was something about Syart's manner that unnerved Lord Edmund, and he drew his sword as a precaution. The castle certainly looked deserted, and an eerie silence echoed imaginary whispers through the castle's empty buildings.

"Tell me, Master Syart," continued Lord Edmund. "how is it that you are walking freely when you should really be locked up?"

"I set him free." A voice that seemed to chill the atmosphere echoed across the castle grounds. Then, after a short while, a hooded figure emerged from one of the buildings near the gatehouse. The figure stood for a moment before throwing back the hood that covered his face.

"Zelfen!" shouted Lord Edmund almost with disbelief, and without thinking of the dangers, he charged. It was a senseless attack and Lord Edmund knew it, because before he could get within striking distance to use his sword, Lord Zelfen sent forth from an outstretched hand a beam of pure energy. Lord Edmund appeared to glow from within. Then, in a mass of blood and bone, he exploded, bursting into a thousand fragments. Movement from within the wagon caused another beam to be directed towards it. The wagon, the horses and Lord Edmund's wife Jaelia were blown into nothingness. The remaining guards, who were terrified at the wanton carnage this one person caused, were trying to control their horses.

"Come to me," called Lord Zelfen as the guards dismounted. "Let me embrace you. Let us put our differences aside and be friends, you and me."

Lord Zelfen's eyes were pits of darkness and the

guards easily fell under his influence. Slowly, one by one, they obeyed their new master.

Lord Tamur, having heard nothing from his father, turned his horse and escorted by the last two guards, made his way towards the village of Tybow. He had heard the two large explosions, and inwardly felt that the worst had happened. He rode away with tears in his eyes.

Lord Zelfen had taken advantage of Lord Edmund's absence from Dronecet Castle and had, with his superior powers, taken control not only of the castle but of the small army that defended it. Sending some soldiers to oblivion proved the point to the others. There were no soldiers looking for Lord Edmund, which was also a lie. They were still within the castle walls under the control and influence of Lord Zelfen, and Lord Zelfen wanted revenge.

Lord Tamur and the two guards who had been ordered to stay with him galloped at speed into the village of Tybow. The horses were hard ridden; white sweat covered their flanks and steam pumped from their nostrils in a steady rhythm. Still a little skittish from the journey, they had to be controlled when villagers gathered round to see who the riders were and why they had come to Tybow. To the puzzlement of the villagers, a guard asked the whereabouts of Aluen of Tybow. There was a murmur within the crowd before one villager came forward to direct the guards to the blacksmith's workshop.

"My thanks, sir" said the guard, and the party proceeded to the Smithy, followed by inquisitive villagers.

Aluen's father was working as usual, and the sounds of hammer against steel echoed through the village. He had been asked by Master Elio to continue working as normal to avoid any suspicion that guests were staying there. He noticed the riders approaching and the small crowd that followed. More business he hoped, but as the riders neared the forge, he recognised Lord Tamur and the fact that he appeared to be distressed for some reason.

"My lord" he began. "I am at your service."

"Thank you, Master Blacksmith." He dismounted and walked into the forge, and when he was out of earshot of the gathering crowd, he whispered in a soft voice. "I must speak to Master Elio urgently."

Aluen's father asked the crowd to disperse, promising them that if there was any news to report he would tell them later. This seemed to satisfy them, and they wandered off in their twos and threes to continue their village life. Master Elio and Master Birch were sitting at the table when Lord Tamur was shown into the room. Cat looked up from her place by the fire, and seeing that no danger threatened, settled down again and was lost in her dreams of Siport and fish.

"I have been expecting you," announced Master Elio.

Lord Tamur was surprised. "You have?"

"Yes, we heard the magic. We saw in our minds what happened at the castle. We are truly sorry, Lord Tamur. Your father, your mother...." He broke off.

Lord Tamur's fears were confirmed. He tried to hold back his emotions.

"You are now elevated to the position of the First Lord of Dronecet Castle, Tamur. I trust that you will act according to the position you now hold." This was not a chastisement by Master Elio, but it was said in a tone that left no doubt as to Lord Tamur's standing, not to mention his future responsibilities in the public eye. Lord Tamur gathered his strength.

"I have two guards with me. The rest I gather have fallen victim to Lord Zelfen's power."

Master Elio asked Aluen's father if he could extend his kindness by allowing the use of the area at the rear of the house as a temporary shelter. He readily agreed, and a canvas was erected to form an extension to the house. The door at the back of the workshop was opened to allow access and to allow warm air to circulate around the shelter. It seemed to make it more habitable. The guards made use of the covered wagon as temporary sleeping quarters, the silver having been taken out and melted into ingots the day after Aluen's homecoming.

That evening when everyone had settled in, a conference was held. All were sitting around the large table in the main room apart from Aluen's mother, who acted as host for the evening; his father worked as usual in the forge until late.

"What will Lord Zelfen be doing?" enquired Aluen.

"Well," began Master Elio, "if we judge from the last confrontation during which many lost their lives, he will be trying to amass troops and form an army. Then he will make an attempt to subdue the land once more. We must try to stop him before he can achieve this. Master Birch will prepare himself, and when he is ready, and only when he is ready, he will find and confront Lord Zelfen. We hope he will be successful, but Lord Zelfen is not a person to be underestimated. He will be expecting Master Birch to challenge him in time, so he too will be preparing for the meeting. It is my belief that Lord Zelfen will try to hurt Master Birch by attacking those close to him. If he becomes distracted, Lord Zelfen will strike with venom unforeseen in this land's history."

Aluen reflected that Lord Zelfen had appeared very kind when they first met. "Is he really that powerful?" he asked. "Is he really that evil?"

"I'm afraid so, my young Master. This is one of

the reasons why Cat is now your companion. If Cat were to be seen with Master Birch, then she might very well become his first target. It might also be known by Lord Zelfen that Master Birch and Cat have the ability to travel within each other, and if Cat were destroyed during this process, Master Birch would cease to exist and the land would be plunged into darkness. It is my hope that you will see the importance of our choices. It will however put you, Master Aluen, in certain danger too."

"Why is that?"

"Well, as we go about our travels together, we will be followed. People other than Lord Zelfen will assume that with Cat as a companion, you are Master Birch. It is our hope that they will give false information as to the whereabouts of the real Master Birch. This will give us time and the advantage. It should draw Lord Zelfen out into the open, so to speak, where Master Birch could confront him with the advantage of surprise."

Aluen, having listened and digested what Master Elio had said, suddenly stood up and threw a goblet to the floor. It was clear that he was upset. "This has been your plan from the beginning, hasn't it?" he said angrily. "You befriend me. Help me with the parchment. Finding the tower and the silver, which to me amounts to blood money, was pre-planned.

Now Cat, who I have become extremely fond of as a result of our meeting, is yet another temptation. Is this why you befriended me in the first place? What if I refuse to help?"

Aluen's mother who had never seen her son angry before, reprimanded him for the outburst in front of his betters.

"Please hear me, Master Aluen," pleaded Master Birch. "We did not take this action lightly and without a great deal of thought. Nor did we try to deceive you. If we went boldly to Dronecet Castle now, then Lord Zelfen would simply transport himself to another place, a safer place. It goes without saying that he would order the soldiers to fight to the death, and they would. There would be many needless casualties. Lord Zelfen is a very evil man, Master Aluen. Such is his power that he might not even be at Dronecet Castle. What is there might just be an image, and this has a tendency to confuse, and before you ask, yes, he has the power to leave spells that could discharge themselves from that image at given targets. We have to make him believe that I am somewhere else. Master Elio and Cat will protect you until death if needs be, but I have to have free movement so that I can locate Lord Zelfen before I act. If I were to attack an image, Lord Zelfen would know immediately where I was and the element of surprise would be lost."

Master Elio walked over to Aluen and rested a hand on his shoulder. "I understand your anger, Master Aluen of Tybow. It must seem that we have wronged you, but please believe me when I say that on no occasion have we meant to deceive or to cause you harm. Have we not demonstrated this by saving your life? Master Aluen, we are but pawns in a universal game of chess. Our fates were sealed at the beginning of time. We are simply instruments, observers and guardians who try, hard as things become, to guide the land and its peoples from falling by the wayside, to keep everyone on the pathway to enlightenment. We did not choose you, Master Aluen. Someone far greater than I had that decision to make, and in my opinion it was a wise choice."

"My parents have been brutally murdered, slain by Lord Zelfen," said Lord Tamur. "He could do this to every family in the land, including yours. Please take - accept - this responsibility, if not for us, for you and your family and friends. Would you have peace of mind if Lord Zelfen were to destroy this land and everyone in it because of your decision not to help in our time of need? Yes it does appear as if the whole scenario was planned beforehand, but would you have agreed at that time? Would you have believed the powers that are at work without being shown some evidence? Why do you think Master Elio occasionally performed little feats of magic for you, if not to demonstrate that it was possible? My father, before surrendering his powers to Master Birch, used magic in his youth to great effect. He told me about the use of magic several times, how it can be heard and how it can use the user if the user is not careful how he applies it. Master Aluen, This land must be free of real magic, for I can see only desolation should it remain."

"Forgive me, gentlemen," replied Master Aluen. "I was being selfish. What would you like me to do?"

"I knew I had picked the right man for the job. Is anyone hungry?" enquired a smiling Master Elio.

Master Aluen had to laugh at his friend's confidence, and soon everyone saw the funny side and peals of laughter could be heard coming from the room, echoing through the night.

A figure who had been listening by the window slowly began to creep away, but not before he had been spotted by Aluen's father. Extremely strong in the arm and with a keen eye, Aluen's father hurled a recently completed horse shoe, which after a few seconds found its mark. Blackness descended, and after dragging the unconscious stranger through the snow, Aluen's father dumped him unceremoniously by the forge and called for Master Elio.

"He was listening by the window, Master Elio."

"And I can see that he accidentally fell over." He

waited until the stranger had regained his senses. "Why were you listening at the window?" he asked.

The stranger could not help but stare into Master Elio's eyes. Those deep wells of knowledge and understanding that invited replies, drew the stranger in, read his mind, then spat it out in disgust.

"He had hoped for a reward in exchange for information," reported Master Elio. "Unfortunately he has just developed a severe case of amnesia and has forgotten all that he thought he heard. You can let him go now."

Once again the spy was dumped unceremoniously in a snow drift, and he sat there for a while complaining to a tree stump.

★ ★ ★

The snows continued for what seemed an age, but eventually, as the cold spell of winter began to lift and the sun warmed the air once more, the snow began to disappear as quickly as it had arrived. Nonetheless this was an even busier period. The melting snows caused the rivers to expand. Great roaring torrents of white-foamed waters raced towards the sea. The owners of grinding mills were extremely happy, because the extra water added speed to the grinding stones, bringing extra output followed by extra profit.

However, not everyone was as jubilant. Some low-lying farmlands were flooded by the extra water as rivers burst their banks, and waterlogged fields delayed the year's planting. Ditches had been dug beforehand to combat this eventuality, but they were not as effective as the farmers had hoped they would be. Many fields were as lakes in the warming sun.

Trees and other plants forced out their new green buds. Flowers in abundance added colour to an otherwise greyish-brown landscape. Birds began to return in their thousands, riding their peculiar v-shaped vehicles. Winds mellowed into warmer breezes and the sun played its warmth across the tree tops. Spring had arrived.

Master Aluen was busy loading his wagon with illusion boxes and various other props, while Master Elio organised the food and water supplies. He was extremely efficient at this task. One of the soldiers had changed out of his uniform and now wore plain robes. He had agreed to travel with the group for part of their journey. The other soldier, after enjoying a blossoming friendship with the blacksmith, had agreed to stay and help him with his work in the forge. He also swore that he would protect the family while Master Aluen was away. This afforded a little comfort in what appeared to be a worsening crisis. Thanking Aluen's father and the family for their winter hospitality, Lord Tamur would travel with Master Elio and Master Aluen for a short while before heading to Castle Tezz.

In the second week of spring, after saying their final goodbyes to family and friends, Master Elio, Master Aluen, Lord Tamur, a soldier and Cat began a journey, a journey that would probably decide the fate of their land and of the people living within it. As the group of friends left the village of Tybow, pans and tools, with the gentle rocking motion, began making their own melody on the side of the wagon and against each other, the metallic beat echoing across the countryside. Unnoticed by all except one, Cat's eyes changed colour from green to ice blue.

CHAPTER EIGHT

"I want to know where Master Birch is hiding. I want that coward found. I am surrounded by imbeciles!" shouted Lord Zelfen.

"It has been impossible because of the snow, my lord. We have searched the Timber Wood and we have scoured the land. We have accomplished as much as we could have done under the circumstances, my lord" stammered a quivering soldier.

As quick as a flash, a red light of eye-piercing brilliance shot forth from Lord Zelfen's outstretched hand. The soldier, with a look of surprise etched on his face, crumbled into dust. A gust of wind blew his remains away. Lord Zelfen began to pace up and down on the parade ground, clenching and unclenching his fists as he cursed under his breath.

"Nothing is impossible!" he screamed. "Do you all want to join the winds of time as specks of dust?"

The remaining soldiers standing on the parade

ground shivered in their fear of what Lord Zelfen would do to them if they were not successful in finding Birch.

"This coward Birch, who dares not face me, is easily recognizable" continued Lord Zelfen. "He travels with a Timber Cat. He is never without that accursed creature. How many people do you see travelling with a Timber Cat for a companion? Find him for me, but beware of his capabilities. He is a formidable opponent. Let me know where he is and I will have the advantage of surprise. I will promise wealth and position to the finder. Go now and commence your searches. Leave no stone unturned!"

Lord Zelfen returned to the warmth of the open fire in the main hall and began a chant that would, he hoped, change the face of the land forever, because sending out the soldiers in search of Birch was only a diversionary tactic. He had other plans.

Syart, his associates and several mounted troops in fear of Lord Zelfen's wrath, immediately began their journey to find Master Birch. It was also Syart's wish that he find Master Aluen; he had a personal score to settle with that young man. They headed towards the village of Tybow, knowing that Aluen's parents lived there. Assuming an air of importance as leader of the group, Syart was also thinking about all the money he could amass with the mounted troops as a back-up. He thought about the position that would inevitably follow should he find Master Birch and bring him in irons to Lord Zelfen.

As the evening drew near, Syart gave orders for a small farmstead on the road to the village of Tybow to be commandeered for his personal use. The occupants were to be forcibly removed and their expected resistance answered with immediate and mindless slaughter. The family was cut to pieces with no sign of remorse from the mindless soldiers, who were still under Lord Zelfen's control.

No one appeared to notice at first. It wasn't just the shadow of evening that crept across the countryside, it was the dark clouds of evil conjured up by Lord Zelfen. They billowed into the lives of all who would welcome them or embrace them as they passed. Lord Zelfen had summoned the ultimate evil. Starting from Dronecet Castle, the clouds began to spread like an avenging mist across the countryside. Snake-like tentacles grasped at every living form. Neighbour turned against neighbour, brother turned against brother, husband against wife. Animals became stricken with terror and turned wild as they fought to escape the advancing mist.

By the following morning the dark cloud had enveloped the farmstead where Syart was lodged. He was sitting at a table counting money, and appraising the valuables that had been taken from the recently-departed occupants. Syart's facial expression had changed that evening. His eyes especially appeared to have bulged, and an evil grin warned the others not to question him, even though they should have done so. According to Lord Zelfen's orders they should have been travelling at this time, but Syart had other plans.

"Tomorrow my friends, tomorrow we shall destroy this village of Tybow and all who live within its boundaries. No stone shall remain unturned in our quest to find Master Aluen. My comrades, think of all the wealth we will glean from their purses." Syart gave an evil laugh, and under the dark spell of the cloud, the others joined in.

Unknown to them as they drank wine until they were virtually incapable of rational thought, was the fact that not all of the original farmstead family had been put to the sword. One small boy had witnessed the slaughter of his parents and family, and at that moment he was running to warn anyone who would listen to his tale. Through the night he had run, tear-stained cheeks leaving streaks down his face. His eyes were still wide with fear. His legs were a criss-crossed pattern of red lines where thorns and brambles had whipped him as he ran. His knees were bleeding after several falls, but still he ran.

The sun was just peeping over the horizon when

the boy entered the village of Tybow. He ran to the meeting place and rang the bell several times before he collapsed, totally exhausted.

A farmer and his wife were the first to arrive at the scene. "What is it, wife?" said the man.

The woman, who was stout and almost typecast in her role as a farmer's wife, lifted the child into her arms. "The poor little thing," she said as she wiped the boy's face with a cloth. "What brings you to our village in such distress, child?"

"'Tis evil ma'am," said the boy and immediately began to cry again.

The farmer rang the bell again to warn the village of a possible threat, and as more people arrived, stories of strange behaviour in the farm animals and dogs began to circulate. Birds too had taken flight after only recently arriving, and an eerie silence was descending over the land.

"What should we do?" asked one of the villagers.

"We should build defences," suggested another.

"And who would fight?" asked Aluen's father, who had recently joined the group. "We are not soldiers, we are farmers and tradesmen, and how many of you could fight something that you cannot see? If my advice is worth anything, we should pack a few necessary things and head for the Border House. We should be safe within its walls."

The village tailor, a tall, gaunt man who was dressed in black robes, stepped forward. "I believe you are all worrying about nothing, and who is afraid of a few thunder clouds anyway? A boy comes to our village with tales of evil, and in less time than it takes to boil an egg, everyone is ready to leave because of what the boy says. It's rubbish, I tell you. The boy has obviously had a bad dream and everyone else has the jitters. It was a dream, wasn't it boy?" He looked directly into the boys eyes.

"Have you ever seen evil, sir?" The boy was still clinging to the farmer's wife. No-one appeared to notice that the boy's face was changing by the minute. His eyes had begun to bulge outwards.

"What kind of stupid question is that? And mind your manners when you speak to your betters." The tailor waved a pair of scissors about to emphasise every word.

"I apologise, Sir. May I see your scissors?" said the boy, whose face had taken on a sinister appearance.

The tailor thinking, that he had proved a point handed the scissors to the boy.

"I asked you, sir, if you had seen evil. Now this is evil," and the boy plunged the scissors into the neck of the farmer's wife.

She let go of the boy almost immediately and stepped backwards. Blood was gushing from the open wound. Eyes that appeared to express a questioning disbelief flickered as she fell backwards to the ground, quite dead. The boy, his eyes now feral in appearance, began laughing hysterically. Then, before anyone had really taken in the enormity of his action, he ran off towards the black cloud that hovered in the distance.

He failed to notice the horse until it was too late. The frightened mare, coat white with frothing sweat and eyes bulging, trampled the boy as it galloped blindly through the village. Within moments the boy lay dead.

Aluen's father called for order. "Those of you who decide to stay here and take their chances with whatever comes, I wish good fortune. As for me, I'm heading for the Border House with anyone who cares to accompany me. I shall be leaving within the hour." He left the crowd of people arguing and headed for his workshop.

In less than an hour a wagon was filled with provisions, the silver ingots safely at the bottom, covered with a canvas sheet. Aluen's mother had never questioned her husband's decisions, and this time was no different as she helped to hitch the horses, check the supplies of food and water and oversee the cooking pots as well as the portable oven. Spare clothes were also stored and kept in a wooden box to prevent dampness. As the final preparations were being carried out, villagers, some riding, some walking, began to arrive at the blacksmith's workshop. The soldier who had stayed to help Aluen's father in the forge began to organise the gathering villagers so that everyone had some form of transport. When all was ready, at a wave of his hand, the villagers slowly moved forward and away from the approaching cloud.

Two days after leaving the village of Tybow, Lord Tamur, with the soldier as guard, left Master Elio and Aluen, and, after making his farewells, headed towards Castle Tezz. Master Elio and Aluen intended to travel the coast road in a bid to further disguise their mission and to head for the village of Arvel by the coast. It was hoped that this might coax Lord Zelfen's spies into making a report.

Lord Zelfen had always considered the North to be his domain; he had even tried to secure it during the war of fifty years before, but he had been defeated. If he received a report that two strangers and a Timber Cat were travelling northward, and he was at Dronecet Castle at the time, he might well have deduced that it was Master Birch and put in a personal appearance. However, as the two companions travelled across country, Master Elio noticed that there was something wrong with the air. There appeared to be a sort of haze in the distance. It was almost like the few moments before a thunderstorm, a sort of foreboding with dark clouds gathering to add effect.

With some difficulty due to the motion of the wagon travelling across open country, Elio stood up for a better view. Holding on to the roof supports, he had his worst fears confirmed. In the distance he saw the black clouds billowing out at ground level. He had heard the magic being performed, a low growl in his ear drums, but he had never expected this even from one as evil as Lord Zelfen. He hurriedly sat down again and began to chant a spell of protection. His voice started with a low grumble, and then like a song, his voice rose and fell in volume in an almost pleading harmony.

Sensing that something was wrong, Master Aluen slowed the wagon and applied the brakes, coming to a stop on a level part of the dirt road. Cat also knew that something was amiss, and appeared restless in the back of the wagon as Master Elio, besides chanting, was making signs with his fingers. His eyes, those pools of knowledge, were covered momentarily by flickering eyelids, and his face too had lost its softness. His skin had stretched tight as though in a fit. After a few moments Master Elio breathed a sigh of relief.

"Don't be alarmed," he announced as though finishing a conversation, "all will be well." He stood again and raised his arms, and as he did so, the sleeves of his robes fell to his elbows. His bare forearms appeared to be alive with miniature lights that were travelling at speed towards his outstretched fingers. Suddenly, two great balls of dazzling brilliance leapt from his fingertips. Master Elio was thrown backwards by the sheer force of the spell, and the lights encircled the wagon and the horses, rising to the height of four men before exploding into a million multi-coloured stars. Slowly the multi-coloured display descended, and with this came a snake-like hissing sound. Then, after the hissing sound could no longer be heard, white steam began to settle over the wagon. Aluen was awestruck, and just a little afraid, as ghostly tentacles of white mist appeared to mummify all that was there. Aluen felt an icy tingle as he breathed in the white mist.

As Master Elio sat down heavily on the wooden bench, the mist began to thin. Then it disappeared altogether.

"What was that all about?"

"We were in mortal danger." Master Elio pointed to the black clouds in the distance.

"Why, because of a thundercloud?"

"It is no ordinary cloud my ignorant friend!" replied Master Elio a little angrily. "That is evil itself, conjured up by none other than Lord Zelfen. Were you to breathe in that filth for any length of time your mind would no longer be your own. The evil in that cloud would eat at you from the inside to the outside. Normal flesh would become a honeycomb of evil that would detest any other living creature and try to kill it. You would fester with sores until you screamed for a release that would not materialise. You would die a horrible death. You will be safe now from its effects, but we still have to make preparations." He thought for a while. "Change of plan. Steer a course for Castle Tezz and pray that we will be there in time. Lord Zelfen will know where I am now. It will not be long before we face danger."

As Aluen steered the horses to the right and released the brakes, the wagon began to move forward.

★ ★ ★

Syart and his men, together with the soldiers, galloped into the village of Tybow, the black cloud billowing just behind them. Infected by the evil in the cloud, they were hardly recognisable from their former selves. Their eyes were bulging and streaked with red lines. Their cheeks had adopted a sunken look, almost skeletal in appearance, and their skin had turned the colour of grey ash. Corpse-like, they assembled at the village green.

One villager who had remained after the others had left with Aluen's father and mother approached Syart, and asked him about his intentions regarding the village and any remaining occupants. Syart's reply came in the form of a length of cold steel which penetrated the villager's chest at shoulder level, and burst out from his back at the waist. Syart lifted his foot from a stirrup, rested it on the villager's shoulder and pushed the still-blinking corpse to the ground.

"Does that answer your question?" laughed Syart in a high-pitched squeal.

An ageing village woman who had already been affected by the cloud sat in a doorway laughing a hideous laugh while at the same time plunging a knife continuously into the body of her dead husband.

"Search for valuables! Kill everyone! Burn the village to the ground!" shrieked Syart.

Suddenly pandemonium broke out in the small village. People were running everywhere. Some were screaming. Some were affected by the madness that burned slowly into their brains. They ran in circles, holding their heads, until death from a sword or lance gave them peace. Others tried to escape, but were faced by the black cloud. Terrified, they fled, only to be caught by the soldiers whose swords and lances dripped crimson with gore.

Syart sat astride his horse and laughed as the fires

were reflected in his black eyes. Overcome with blood lust, he joined in the massacre, his high-pitched laughter echoing throughout the burning village. It was the last sound some of the villagers heard before death gave them peace from the carnage. Other villagers who had stayed behind were engulfed in flames as one by one the inferno consumed the tinder-dry buildings. Clouds of smoke filled the steadily darkening sky as Syart, apparently satisfied for the time being, rode slowly out of what had been the village of Tybow and headed South. His men and the soldiers followed and with them, laden with the wealth of the village, was a cart pulled by two horses.

★ ★ ★

After two weeks of hard travelling, Master Elio, Aluen and Cat reached Castle Tezz. The journey was not without incident. On several occasions Master Elio, as a protection against anyone who might have been affected by the dark cloud, cast spells and sent anyone approaching the wagon back from whence they came. This was merely a preventive measure. He did not want to punish anyone unnecessarily by inviting them to visit Dronecet Castle, so he simply sent them back to their starting point. One merchant, who had travelled by foot from Penste Harbour, was totally bewildered that he had spent twenty-eight days travelling, acquiring very sore feet, without actually getting anywhere. A few ladies who had been enjoying the occasional freedoms that merchants' wives were granted due to their husband's occupation, had a great deal to explain when their men arrived home unexpectedly.

Master Elio, pondering upon the many scenarios that his actions had created, giggled to himself as the wagon passed through the gates of Castle Tezz. The wagon came slowly to a halt and Aluen climbed down to stretch himself; it had been a long and tiring journey. He was elated to find that his parents, after receiving advice from the commander of the Border House, had recently arrived and were safe from harm. He embraced them both as tears of happiness ran down his cheeks. Master Elio nodded his head in acknowledgement as he passed and went directly to the main hall to join Lords Karl, Torran and Tamur. Cat followed and lay down by the large open fire while discussions echoed in an otherwise silent hall.

"We have a problem," began Master Elio. "Lord Zelfen has used a most powerful spell and one which could end civilisation as we know it. He has created a black cloud which multiplies by itself and is without doubt totally evil. At this moment it surrounds Dronecet Castle and reaches even to the village of

Tybow. Anyone, and I repeat anyone who enters this black cloud, this vile abhorrence, will be subject to mind change and will attack anything and everyone, even those who have been already affected in the same way. We appear, gentlemen, to be in a no-win scenario. We cannot attack Dronecet Castle, where I am sure Lord Zelfen is hiding; the result would be catastrophic. Our forces would be affected by the cloud, and in all probability they would turn against us and each other. I could not give protection to an invading force even if I wanted to. There would be far too many men for me to hold an enchantment together.

"The worst part of this is, they have the ability to attack us. Lord Zelfen has obviously thought long and hard about the use of this spell. It appears, gentlemen, that all we can do at this point is to defend ourselves and hope that the black cloud remains where it is. Unless anyone has any ideas?"

"We have been getting reports of limited engagements from the Border House." Lord Karl was pacing the hall.

"You must send word to your forces that under no circumstances are they to enter that cloud" replied Master Elio.

Lord Karl summoned a messenger, and after a few moments had passed during which a letter was drafted, he handed it to the messenger.

"Take this directly to the Border House Commander. Keep to the woods and fields and away from the regular routes, and under no circumstances should you enter any black clouds, however inviting."

The messenger saluted before speeding away.

Lord Torran had said little; he was pondering several scenarios. "You said that the black cloud has already reached the village of Tybow, Master Elio. Is it still growing?"

"Not at this point. It looks as if it has stopped for the time being."

"But what if it decides to start growing again?"

"I'm not altogether sure that it can. Lord Zelfen has created the cloud, but it feeds on evil and multiplies by itself. Let me try to explain. If I were evil, or had any evil intent within me and I stood just one yard away from the cloud, it would in all probability move forward to encompass me. You might deduce that it wanted me to join with it, but that would not be the case. It would take me in, extract all the evil, supply me with new evil and spit me out in far worse condition than I was in in the first place. It might be that it has reached its full extent, and in that case Lord Zelfen has prepared his ground well. He will now invite anyone to try to reach him on his own terms, and at the same time they will have to defend themselves against the cloud and the things that emerge from within it. Eventually the cloud will consume everything we send before we even reach Lord Zelfen. We would have lost before we even start."

"Then we have already lost," remarked Lord Karl.

"I didn't say that," continued Master Elio. "We still have time on our side. For the moment, the only way to proceed is for our forces to protect the Border House and Castle Tezz. Limit the range of the patrols to within one day's ride of the cloud, and make doubly sure that no one with evil intent gains access to the stronghold. This, I am sure you will understand, will only invite the cloud. Master Aluen has protection against the effects of the cloud and so does Cat. Let them be our eyes and ears in our search for a remedy and in our search for Lord Zelfen."

"Hold on a minute" interrupted Lord Tamur. "How can one boy and a cat be expected to fight their way through the cloud, and then if they find Lord Zelfen, confront him too? It can't be done."

"He will not be expected to do much other than to drive the wagon. Look at Cat for a moment, especially notice her eyes."

After everyone had observed that Cat's eyes were ice blue, a murmur of agreement closed the subject.

Master Elio continued. "I'm not sure, but I don't think Lord Zelfen quite knows the capabilities of Master Birch and Cat, and I am sure you will concur that this is to our advantage. Even Master Aluen, sharp as he is, hasn't noticed. A small but necessary spell, you will agree."

"Do you not think," remarked Lord Tamur "that we should ask Master Aluen if he would undertake such a perilous journey, rather than take it for granted that he will?"

"We are running ahead of ourselves," said Lord Karl. He summoned a guard to act as a messenger, and gave instructions to locate Aluen and ask him if he would join the group at his convenience.

The messenger was away for several minutes before Aluen came into the hall. He looked terribly young as he bowed gracefully to the lords.

"He's been practising," said Master Elio with a broad grin.

"Master Aluen," began Lord Karl, choosing his words carefully. "It appears from reports given by Master Elio that you are immune from the effects of the black cloud."

"Thanks to Master Elio I believe I am, my lord."

Lord Karl began to fidget. He couldn't think how to ask a straightforward question to someone who really did not deserve this kind of responsibility.

"Of course I will go." Aluen had guessed the unspoken question.

"I told you he has been practising," smiled Master

Elio. "I believe that has answered the question. An armed escort will accompany Master Aluen and Cat on their journey as far as they are able. The escort will then wait at a pre-appointed location while Master Aluen continues into the cloud to gather information. I shall remain here in case I am needed."

Aluen looked concerned for a moment. "If you are not to travel with me, how will I be able to fight Lord Zelfen if he confronts me?"

Master Elio reassured him. "Have no fear, young Master Aluen. I would not allow you to go if I thought you might come to harm. Everything will become clearer to you in good time. I suggest that you commence your journey tomorrow morning. This will allow time for preparation, parting speeches, a decent meal and plenty of rest."

Aluen spent part of that evening with his parents, and before retiring he told them of his intended journey. He told them where he would travel and what he had volunteered to do during the journey. He emphasised that he would be safe and protected by Master Elio. Later that evening Aluen's parents stood on the balcony adjoining their rooms. His father's eyes were brimming with tears.

"Our boy has grown up somewhat," he remarked, as he gazed into a cloudless sky.

The moon looked more rounded that night. It was

like a red-tinted globe hanging on a curtain of black satin, and silver stars twinkled in their thousands. The countryside, unusually quiet except for the barking of farmyard dogs, appeared at peace as Aluen's father, comforted by his wife, wept out his frustration in the solitude of their rooms. In another part of the castle, in an isolated room far away from busy corridors, Master Elio, along with Birch, began to chant. Every avenue of magic was checked and double-checked. Every possible loophole was investigated and sealed with magic. The wagon in which Aluen would travel had been covered with tiny rune markings. This was a war of a different kind from that of fifty years ago; it was a war of spell and counter-spell. It was chess-like, and each move had to be covered, every opening protected. Master Elio was about to move his King's pawn to King's four.

CHAPTER NINE

Syart and his army of followers, blinded by the evil that continuously multiplied within their weakening bodies, were now quite mad as they travelled, almost purposely, towards the South. Their hair was greasy and matted against their scalps. Their eyes were bulbous, with prominent red veins and pink sockets. Insane smiles stretched tight across their faces, and their skin, an ash grey, had begun to break out into boils and open sores. It was as though they were slowly being consumed by the evil within the cloud; eaten alive piece by piece.

This was Lord Zelfen's only mistake so far. He had failed to realise that mere mortals could not endure such evil inner forces, and eventually, even if they could survive a battle, those forces would be their downfall. They would wither away into nothingness like maggot-infested carcasses.

They passed through Forest Town without

acknowledging its existence. People stood and watched as the small army passed by. The smiling horsemen made the townsfolk feel uncomfortable, because they looked neither to right nor left. It was as though they were on a mission and had to be somewhere other than this town which was of little significance to them.

Seldom stopping, even for a rest which they didn't seem to need, Syart and his small band of followers finally approached the Forest of Frezfir, where they could go no further on horseback. They dismounted, and for a moment they wandered about, their still-smiling faces looking at the trees. The forest seemed to invite them in, and an unspoken word urged them to enter. Although faces were stretched into smiles, some eyes were brimming with tears.

Syart, suddenly childlike, began scampering around, hugging at tunics, pulling hair and prodding bodies with his sword.

"Catch me if you can, ha ha!" he laughed in a squeaky voice as he ran toward the edge of the forest. "First one to catch me gets stabbed. Ha ha!"

Then he disappeared into the forest and was lost amongst the trees and bushes. The rest of the small army hesitated, but only for a moment. As though encouraged by Syart's actions, his men, as well as the soldiers, drew their swords. Leaving the wagon loaded with valuables by the roadside, they ran laughing into the forest after their leader. There were no rules to this strange game; people simply died laughing.

"Got you, ha ha!" yelled Syart as he thrust his sword into an unsuspecting soldier. The smiling soldier looked at Syart, laughed back and died.

Syart quickly looked around, checked for targets, and then scampered off again deeper into the forest. The peals of laughter echoed through the trees and sent the forest wildlife scattering in all directions. It was as though some higher force had steered Syart and his men to this destination in order that they could play their final game together, their game of death. As time slowly passed, the laughter began to dwindle, the shrieks of surprise faded. The last man laughed and fell on his own sword, and there was silence. This was a strange silence, a sort of anti-sound before the many natural forest noises resumed their cacophony of insect and animal conversation.

★ ★ ★

To keep a low profile, Aluen journeyed towards the east coast without an escort. It was more natural and the route least likely to encounter hostilities. It was a wide, flat road that offered no cover for would-be ambushers. Armies could be seen from a good distance, so the eastern route was the best and safest way. He considered an escort to be too obvious, and it would attract attention. In fact he had made no detailed plans for the journey at all. He had simply said before his departure that he would find his own way by travelling towards the village of Arvel. When he reached this village he would turn west and head directly into the darkness of the strange black cloud.

To keep Castle Tezz informed as to his whereabouts and to pass on information regarding his journey, Aluen had taken with him six birds which had been trained to fly back to Castle Tezz. Each bird had also been given a spell of protection from Master Elio to ensure the flow of information. On the legs of these birds Aluen could attach messages and information of importance, and this would keep Lord Karl up to date on his progress, his needs and in the worst-case scenario, it would give the lords time to prepare themselves, according to the seriousness of the situation.

Aluen journeyed for a few days in an easterly direction, and then followed the River Zarh. After he had been travelling for twelve days without any major problems, he came to the Lake of Dreams and crossed over towards the east coast road. Cat for the most part had remained in the back of the covered wagon, its canvas shielding her from prying eyes. Only now and then would she leap out and stretch herself, secretly surveying the area in the process, then, satisfied that all was as it should be, she would jump back into the wagon and resume her half-sleep.

As the coast road came into view, the Sea of Winds blew its damp mist of welcome across it. The air, although damp, was crisp and fresh, and the cry of seagulls filled the grey morning sky. Cat was walking in great strides alongside the wagon and leaving impressions of her great paws in the moist sand at the road's edge.

It was at this time that Aluen spotted the first of many strange-looking people on this journey, people with a host of different facial expressions, many of them with fixed smiles. It was as though the expressions were carved into the architecture of each body. None of these people seemed to show any sign of acknowledgement, nor did they appear to notice Cat, who was very wary of these peculiar beings. Seemingly non-violent, they all walked as though in a trance and all in the same direction. Aluen tried his best to ignore this strange sight, although it was, to say the least, a little unnerving.

When he had made camp for the night, many were seen to pass by without so much as a glance in his direction. This was a silent army of souls with a single purpose, to continue their journey, just as Aluen was continuing his. Aluen would have liked to know where these people were going so he could make a report, but although he called several times to them, none answered his questions. He decided to send a description of the scene to Lord Karl at Castle Tezz, and having done so he continued his journey.

There were people who knew exactly where these strange people were going. The inhabitants of Penste Harbour were overcome by the numbers and astonished by the weird, even comical-looking people entering their town. They came from Arvel, from Holb and from the many small settlements that lined the coastal regions. They even came from as far away as Leith. This strangely silent army passed through the town of Penste Harbour and then, without so much as a whisper, they walked straight into the sea. None returned.

When he was nearing the Timber Wood, Aluen made camp for the night. While he was building a campfire Cat's eyes changed colour from ice-blue to green, then, after only a few minutes, back to ice-blue. During those few minutes Master Birch, while shielding his magic, had transported himself to the little log-built cabin in the Timber Wood, and after making sure that everything was in order, he returned unnoticed by anyone, including Aluen.

It was not until Aluen had covered almost half his

journey along the east coast road and was near to the village of Arvel, that one or two passing strangers showed signs of hostility towards him. These people were different from those previously encountered, in that they appeared to have more control over their actions and could make decisions. Their facial expressions were also different. This new group's faces were not fixed in a smile, although they appeared to grin a lot.

Aluen wondered what would happen if a group of them stopped him on the road. Would they attack him? Amongst his supplies, he had a bow and a small sword just in case, but they would be of little comfort to him and little use if a number of these people attacked.

He turned to look at Cat and felt a lot better. What did surprise him, considering that there might be a war to fight in the fullness of time, was that there was a complete absence of preparation for such an event. There were no groups of soldiers to be seen, no checkpoints or lookouts posted. There was not even a supply wagon to be seen, and these were the lifeline of any army. This was an enigma that troubled him.

The only hostile actions came from passers-by. At first the abuse was only verbal, but the closer he got to the black cloud, the more hostile people became. He could see that there would come a time when he would have to protect himself, and his defences were few. He wrote a message to Lord Karl at Castle Tezz and attached it to one of the birds before allowing it to fly away.

Sire
I find no indication that
armies are assembling.
I have seen no hostile troop
 movements. I shall be travelling
in a westerly direction at daybreak.

Your Servant
Aluen of Tybow

The bird flew up into the early evening sky. It circled once and then flew southward to Castle Tezz.

Master Elio and the other lords were sitting around a large wooden table in the main hall at Castle Tezz. They were being served with late evening refreshments when a guard entered the room bearing the message sent by Aluen. Lord Karl read the message aloud to the rest of the assembly.

"What do you make of it?" he asked.

"I don't know" began Lord Torran. "It's obvious that on the face of this evidence, Lord Zelfen is trying a different approach. There have been small skirmishes around the Border House district, but nothing that might be considered as a military action. It's that black cloud that puzzles me."

"Perhaps I might have an answer." Master Elio held up a chicken leg. "When the last battle was fought Lord Zelfen was defeated, and not solely by Master Birch. He will have learned valuable lessons from that meeting. What I mean to say is, he fought that battle using magic. He covered an immense area of land and sea, and employed a large number of renegades by manipulating each one with his powers, men on land and men at sea in ships. When he confronted Master Birch, he was weakening. You have to remember that at that time Master Birch had only recently gained his full powers. He was a novice in comparison to Lord Zelfen, a fortunate one but still a novice. Now this time Lord Zelfen appears to be conserving his powers;, he has learned by his mistake. If he defeats Master Birch when they meet, there will be no one to stand in his way and prevent him from ruling Modania. May the gods forbid this to happen!

"The black cloud is evil itself and once conjured, it can sustain itself by feeding off the evil in others. I have to admit that I feel for the safety of Master Birch if Lord Zelfen has his powers at full strength."

"What if we were to send an army to keep Lord Zelfen busy and his mind off Master Birch?" Lord

Karl was thinking of possible military avenues of attack.

"Where would they go? Who would they fight?" Master Elio saw the futility of the suggestion. "It wouldn't make a feather breadth of difference if you were to send every one of your fighting soldiers. All you would succeed in doing would be to get all of your soldiers infected by the cloud. No, it can't be done that way. This has to be left to Master Birch. I have done all that I can, and all that you can do now is to pray to the gods and hope for a miracle."

The lords ate the rest of their evening meal in an uneasy silence. It did not seem to be natural to let just one person fight a war, when there were so many able-bodied men who were willing to march at a moment's notice. It was the frustration of the inability to do anything that grated on their minds.

★ ★ ★

Master Aluen had had a troubled night and sleep did not come easily. The only thing he could think of was the black cloud which continued to grow and billow in the distance. What would happen when he entered it? Would the numerous spells worked by Master Elio and Master Birch really prevent him from becoming infected, like those he had seen during his journey?

The black cloud played on his mind and reminded him of the huge thunder clouds of his boyhood when he used to run into his mother's arms for protection. "The gods are angry today," his mother used to say.

After being comforted he used to sit on his mother's knee and watch the displays as forked lightning streaked across the grey sky. Then the rains came, slowly at first, then as the heavens opened up, torrents of rain came down to make miniature streams in the roadway.

"Now the gods are crying for someone," his mother would add as great tears of rain splashed onto the ground, and when the rain stopped and the sun shone through a multi-coloured rainbow, his mother told him of the gods' treasure which could be found at the end of the great archway of colour.

The memories seemed to cheer him somewhat as he made a small fire on which to heat his breakfast of sliced meats. Cat stood by as if in assurance that all would be well. As Aluen began to eat his breakfast, Cat's eyes widened, her ears pricked up and she bounded away into the misty morning. Aluen was too busy eating to notice anything, and he certainly didn't hear what Cat heard. He thought Cat had gone to exercise her muscles after being cooped up in the wagon for so long.

There were five altogether. Their features made it

evident that they had been infected by the black cloud. Their eyes bulged outward and their faces were hollow and dark, sunken to the bone and skeletal. They were sitting in a circle; a small pile of valuables was placed at the centre. To their right and at the bottom of a small embankment were two lifeless bodies.

"See what those two nice gentlemen have left us," gloated one of the men.

Cat was lying close to the ground, just as she would if she were hunting. She watched the men until an itch on her nose made her sneeze. She stood up, a dark silhouette against the morning sky and was noticed by the five men, who also stood up.

"Look here men," called one of the five. "It appears we have meat for breakfast."

"And a warm fur for the cold nights," added another.

As though by silent command, the five men began to spread out. They drew their swords and slowly encircled Cat. But then, in the hazy morning mist, a blue nimbus appeared to surround her.

"What's this then?" asked one of the men.

The answer was quite unexpected. Intense light shot forth from Cat's eyes and within seconds the forest had returned to silence once more. Cat returned to Aluen's campsite just as he was making ready to travel again. She jumped into the back of the wagon to purr drum rolls of contentment.

The journey was becoming too simple, thought Aluen, as he was aware of no further incidents. It was something that made him feel a little uneasy. Surely there would be obstacles in place, or some kind of resistance? Perhaps an ambush, he thought. Nothing but an eerie silence travelled with them - until they came face to face with the black mass.

Thunder appeared to come from within the black cloud, and flashes of sheet lightning periodically showed its brilliance. Aluen watched for several minutes before the cloud appeared to give way as he steered the wagon into it. The horses, which had been charmed by Master Elio and Birch, did not seem to notice any change, but Aluen was startled by the view he beheld. To the front was a greyness that was difficult to comprehend, and to the rear a black curtain of billowing cloud closed behind him. This was a strange place, where the land looked totally lifeless. Nothing was growing there and the trees, or what remained of them, were covered with dark brown and black fungi. No birds sang their sweet melodies in this greying wilderness, but there were whispers that Aluen could not understand. It was as though the wind was trying to speak to him in this dense atmosphere and the meaning was lost amid the blackness.

The few farmsteads he passed were uninhabited, mere shells of their former grandeur, and the rotting carcasses of once-proud buildings were a stark reminder of a once thriving community. Broken carts, tools, stalls and workshops, all ghost-like, echoed their busy past.

On the second day after crossing the River Ketan, he entered a small settlement where he hoped there might be someone to talk to, but it was just another ghost town. Doors and windows were left open as though the occupants were expecting to return, but only silence greeted him.

Aluen slowed the wagon and stopped at the village centre. This was where under normal circumstances he would deliver the news to the gathering village folk, and perhaps with their consent he would put on a demonstration of his skills as an illusionist. Aluen had never been witness to such a total silence and it made him feel uneasy; he longed for conversation.

Suddenly, Cat's ears twitched. She moved her huge head to one side as though listening.

"What's the matter, Cat?" he whispered.

Cat leapt from the wagon and cautiously approached one of the derelict houses.

"Who's out there?" called a voice from within the house. "Leave me alone!"

Aluen's heart skipped a beat. "Hello!" he called.

"I'm Master Aluen of Tybow. Who are you?"

The door to the house opened slightly, and a young face peered out and looked directly at Aluen. It was a girl! Rounded and rosy cheeks smiled invitingly and added colour to the otherwise, grey surroundings.

"Are you not affected by the black cloud?" she called.

"No" replied Aluen as he jumped down from the wagon.

"How is it that you are not affected?" she called.

The door of the house opened wide, and the prettiest young girl Aluen had ever seen came out and stood by the roadside. She was wearing a plain white smock and wore sandals on her feet. Her hair fell about her shoulders and she stood hands behind her back, in a seductive pose. Aluen's heart was lost to this vision of beauty, and he began to walk towards her.

"You never answered my question" she smiled. "How is it that you are not affected by the black cloud?"

Before he could answer there was a flurry of movement as Cat suddenly leapt at the girl and knocked her to the ground. Aluen was stunned.

"Stop that Cat!" he shouted. "Stop it! She's not affected by the cloud."

The girl sat up, but something was changing. Her voice had a deep throaty rasp to it. "Of course I'm infected, you stupid boy. Your animal knows better than you."

The vision of beauty that Aluen had beheld a few moments ago suddenly began to change. The girl's hair turned to matted grey slime, and her face erupted into sores and boils. She held a long knife in her hand, and after awkwardly standing up, she began to approach Aluen with an evil grin on her face.

"I asked you once before. Now I'll ask you again and I want an answer. How is it that you are not affected by the black cloud?"

Again before Aluen could answer, a beam of light from Timber Cat's eyes struck the girl full in her chest. A look of surprise showed on her face as she slowly melted into the ground. Only a few tattered rags bore witness to where she had been.

Cat padded over to where Aluen stood, shocked at what he had just witnessed. He looked at Cat, and suddenly he could hear a voice. It was not a spoken voice but one that entered his mind.

He is looking for weakness.
If you had given over the
knowledge of how you
were protected,
he would have found
a way to destroy you.

"Who is that?" called Aluen, but the voice was gone. The only sound remaining was the occasional clash of thunder. "Come on, Cat, let's get moving or you will be talking to me next" he called.

He climbed back onto the wagon and released the brake before slowly moving away. Cat jumped into the back and Aluen increased his speed.

CHAPTER TEN

Master Elio, deep in thought was pacing the floor of the main hall. He was muttering calculations and chuckling to himself while the other lords stood about watching attentively.

"He can't lose!" shouted Master Elio triumphantly.

"And how did you arrive at that conclusion?" enquired Lord Karl.

"Right," continued Master Elio. "Do you remember the first battle between Lord Zelfen and Master Birch, when it appeared that Lord Zelfen had lost the battle through weakness?"

The lords nodded, but were not sure of the direction in which Master Elio was going.

"That was only a small factor, but it was more than that."

"Yes but…" interrupted Lord Torran.

"Yes but…" continued Master Elio. "Let us look

at this problem using mathematical calculation. A plus minus a plus gives a minus where the minus indicates a fight. A minus plus a minus still gives a minus where the plus equals a fight. A plus minus a minus gives a plus. Don't you see?"

The lords stared blankly in Master Elio's direction.

"No, you don't see. Look, its universal mathematics. If two people of high but equal rank fight a duel, there can be no winners. Even the victor actually loses. He loses friendships, respect and even money if he has to pay for the loser's funeral. He may also have to pay for the defeated gentleman's household, a large sum of money to compensate for their loss. Plus minus plus equals minus. If two people of low status have a fight they also lose respect and probably the chance of promotion. Minus plus a minus equals minus. Now then, when two opposites fight there is always a winner. Plus minus a minus must therefore equal a plus. It's so easy. A lord dispatches a renegade and he commands respect, so he wins. A renegade despatches a lord who is a tyrant and he gets to be hanged, but he wins respect and becomes a martyr to his own peer group. He wins, don't you see?"

"Master Elio, please," interrupted Lord Karl. "Do you think you could explain that theory in understandable language?"

"He will win, mathematically speaking," assured Master Elio. "Well I think he will win." He sat down and began counting on his fingers.

Aluen recognised Dronecet Castle from a distance, and as he drew near he could see the grey stone walls rising out of a dirty mist that hugged the ground. He remembered how it was when he had attended the mystic fair. The colours were vivid in his mind and contrasted with what he now saw before him. He remembered the smell of the food cooking on open fires and the happiness of all those who had attended. He remembered that he had found a parchment, the same parchment that had ultimately led him to this destination, and sitting on the wagon he wished it could have been different. He looked towards the battlements where so many flags had danced in the wind, and where soldiers on watch duty had waved to the people below. The battlements were deserted now and left to the memories of the past.

As Aluen followed the road around to the castle entrance, a sense of foreboding came over him; there was fear in the pit of his stomach. The drawbridge was down. which surprised him, and the castle gates were open wide. It appeared to be an invitation, but Aluen wasn't in the least bit tempted to take the wagon inside the castle.

"Wait here," said a voice behind him. Aluen spun around to see that Master Birch was sitting alongside Cat in the back of the wagon.

"How did you get here so quickly? Have you been following me?"

"You might say that I have been close for your entire journey," Birch grinned. "This is my journey from this point on. You have done your father proud and we owe you a debt of gratitude. Go now, with my blessing." Birch jumped down from the wagon, leaving Cat in a half-sleep.

Aluen turned the wagon and moved slowly away, but after travelling only a short distance he stopped the wagon and applied the brake. After climbing down and surveying the area he began to make a camp fire.

"I haven't come all this way for nothing," he said aloud. "I shall wait here for your return."

Footsteps echoed in the silence as Master Birch walked across the drawbridge and into the castle grounds. There he sat on the stone steps which led to the battlements. For a while he concentrated before beginning to chant a spell of protection. A few moments later, a blue nimbus and a million miniature stars surrounded him. He was ready. He walked to the centre of the deserted parade ground.

"Lord Zelfen!" he shouted. "I am Master Birch of the Timber Wood. I have come to settle our business."

His voice echoed throughout the deserted castle, and could be heard in every room and along every corridor. Birch walked toward the main castle buildings. "Lord Zelfen!" he shouted again as he moved to examine the next room. That, too, was empty and he began to wonder if Lord Zelfen was really in the castle.

He began a systematic search of all the rooms. He checked the store rooms and the armoury, the kitchen and the reception rooms before arriving at the main hall. He threw open the doors, to be met by a blast which knocked him to the ground. He quickly recovered and ran into the hall, but it was deserted. Lord Zelfen had disappeared.

"Lord Zelfen!" shouted Birch. "Are we to play games?"

Birch retraced his steps and further checked each room as he made his way back towards the gate house. As he neared the gate house, the ground before him exploded in a shower of black sparks. Lord Zelfen stood in the centre of the parade ground, preparing for another strike. Birch held forth his hand and light burst from his fingertips, but it was not quick enough. Lord Zelfen had vanished before the spell could take effect.

'So,' thought Birch. 'He has been hiding here studying the castle. He must know every corner by now.' He ran across to the stables, checked every stall, then double-checked the hay loft and storage compartments. The place was deserted except for the lingering smell of horses. He sat down on a bale of hay and began to chant a spell of concealment and discovery to aid his search. When he had completed the spell, he looked through the third eye created by the spell and found Lord Zelfen to be in an upstairs room. He made his way there by way of the long corridor that ran along the side of it, but before he could catch up, Lord Zelfen moved from the room and headed to the master bedroom. He had sensed the presence of Birch, but could not see him; he just knew he was there.

Suddenly, out of what appeared to be thin air, came a brilliant red fireball which smashed into Lord Zelfen before he could translocate himself again. He was knocked to the ground, his robes smouldering.

Master Birch moved swiftly so as not to present a target and transported himself to the soldiers' billets on the ground floor. Lord Zelfen was furious. He stood up, his robes smothered with glowing embers from Birch's attack. He ran to the stairs which led to the battlements and hurriedly climbed them. He was about to look for Birch in that area when he noticed the wagon, the horses and Aluen in a shaded area near the river. He laughed out loud and quickly transported himself to the area.

Birch felt the vibrations of the spell and ran to the main gates just in time to see Lord Zelfen materialise by the wagon, but Birch didn't move from the main gates; he just smiled. Aluen was frightened and backed up to the wagon, just as Cat looked out. She bared her teeth as Lord Zelfen spoke.

"So Master Aluen of Tybow, we meet again. Have you spent all of your fortune in silver that you have to act as a chaperon to an oversized beast and a freak of nature? I know you are watching, Master Birch, I can feel your presence behind me. Watch now as your chaperon burns!"

Lord Zelfen raised his hand, and like a pencil travelling in a straight line across paper a grey bolt of energy shot forth from his outstretched fingers. Aluen threw his hands across his face in a bid to protect himself, but so did Lord Zelfen as the spell rebounded. Cat followed the returning spell in a movement that was a blur, but Lord Zelfen managed to transport himself again before the spell, followed by Cat, connected to him.

Cat returned to the wagon as Master Birch smiled a knowing smile. It was also a smile of relief that Master Elio's spells and rune signs had worked. He ran back to the castle in pursuit of Lord Zelfen, who had materialised on the battlements again. Immediately he sent a red beam of light, which Lord

Zelfen only just managed to avoid by moving swiftly to the parade ground. He was consumed with rage as he faced Master Birch.

"It's time to stop playing games, Lord Zelfen!" shouted Birch. "You have raped this land. You have turned brother against brother and infected them with a vile disease. You are betrothed to an evil which has brought with it a pestilence to disfigure and to destroy. It all stops here."

"Who are you to call me?" shouted Lord Zelfen. "You with your fancy ideas of a utopia! You have gone soft. You pretend that all is sweetness and light, but this isn't reality, Master Birch. I am the only reality, and I will be your worst nightmare." A black nimbus began to glow around him. "Come, Master Birch, and I will show you that I can do anything I want to in this land. Come and meet your realities!"

Master Birch walked slowly to the parade ground, a blue nimbus protectively surrounded him.

"You couldn't even cast a spell on the mere mortal form of Master Aluen, Lord Zelfen. You ran away in case you got hurt by your own folly."

"Just wait until I have dispatched your ugly form to a place of everlasting torture. I will make Master Aluen my servant, and his first task will be to kill and prepare that accursed beast of yours for my dinner."

Lord Zelfen threw another black line of death

towards Birch. The spell glanced off the protective blue nimbus and went harmlessly to earth.

"Is that all you are capable of?" Birch mocked Zelfen as he held out his hands. "Ice!" he called, and as bidden millions of ice pellets bombarded Lord Zelfen until he was completely encased in a block of freezing particles. "Had you forgotten my extra powers, Lord Zelfen? I hadn't."

The oversized ice cube exploded outwardly in a thousand pieces, and Lord Zelfen shivered as he sent an answering spell hurtling towards Birch. Birch commanded Wind and Water, and the wind answered by bending Lord Zelfen's spell. It harmlessly disintegrated, but Lord Zelfen was drenched as a sheet of water fell on him. According to plan, Birch could see that Lord Zelfen was becoming infuriated, and he laughed out loud to add insult to injury.

"I didn't think you wanted to play games," screamed a red-faced Lord Zelfen.

Master Birch was looking for an opening in Lord Zelfen's defences, a crack in his armour. Both knew that the opening spells were designed to disorientate the opponent, and Lord Zelfen was losing.

"Earth and Stone!" shouted Birch, and the ground where Lord Zelfen stood began to move. Small stones pelted his face, and he almost lost his footing when the ground beneath him began to roll like a wave on the ocean.

"Stop this! Fight like a man!" he screamed. "I shall overcome you, Master Birch. I shall…"

His words were cut short as he fell over, much to his opponent's amusement. Standing up again and balancing on the rolling ground, he was beyond anger.

"I shall unmake you Birch. You will cease to exist!"

"You cannot do that" he replied. "No-one can produce that spell, it is forbidden."

"I can do whatever I like. I am Lord Zelfen. I am a god. You will never take my place, never. I shall rule the world!"

Suddenly he stood rigidly upright. He lowered his head and began to chant the spell of unmaking, a chant forbidden even to the gods, for nature itself would exact a terrible revenge.

"No, Zelfen!" shouted Birch. "Not this way, it can't be completed. Don't do this!"

But Lord Zelfen was almost hysterical with anger and did not seem to realise what he was actually contemplating before it was too late. He threw back his head and held out both hands, and then at the top of his voice he shouted the command.

"Be not, Master Birch of the Timber Wood!"

Suddenly there came a threatening silence, an anti-sound punctuated only by a cracking that was followed by a low rumble in the distance. Lord Zelfen began to laugh hysterically as he felt the power of the spell.

Birch wasted little time and ran out of the castle to where Master Aluen and Cat were waiting.

"Take cover my friends."

"What's the matter?" asked Aluen.

"I think Lord Zelfen has gone mad. He believes that he can unmake things and I feel sorry for him."

"I don't understand."

"When something is made, it is made from the billions of atoms in the universe. There is a fine natural balance, and each thing made takes its place in the grand scheme of things. If someone tries to unmake something, there is no place for the atoms to go. You can't put something in a place where it doesn't fit and so the spell rebounds onto the maker. Nature itself takes revenge on the person trying to disturb its balance. Well it's something like that."

"Oh…" Aluen was about to ask a further question when the ground before them began to vibrate. The rumbling, mixed with Lord Zelfen's laughter, became louder, and the skies answered with the echo of its own bass drums. Thunder sounded and stretched fingers of lightning streaked across the heavens. Lord Zelfen could hardly stand. He began to realise that the spell was unachievable; it was turning in on itself.

"This can't happen," he screamed. "I am a god! I am all powerful and nothing can harm a god, nothing!"

He began to laugh again, but his mind was collapsing. Around the castle there started a whining noise. It was not unlike the sound of a swarm of bees, but much louder.

Then the first beam of light exploded from the sky. It struck Lord Zelfen in the chest and held him rigid, and was followed by a second beam of light, and then a third. Multi-coloured beams flashed in every direction and held him aloft. He was floating, his feet dangling two feet from the ground, and he was shaking as though in a fit. He tried to shout words of appeasement. He tried spells of cancellation and protection, but it was too late; nature would have her pound of flesh.

Lord Zelfen saw the beam of white light energy coming to him from a distance and screamed for forgiveness. He never finished what he was saying. As the beam hit him, there was a tremendous explosion of sound and light. Miniature stars exploded in an array of multi-coloured splendour. Then there was silence. Lord Zelfen was no more.

It began to rain small droplets of clean water, and the black cloud appeared to dissolve, leaving the land fresh and ready to grow again. Master Birch, Master Aluen and Cat stood up from their makeshift shelters and looked around.

"Is it all over now?" asked Aluen.

"Yes, I believe it is, my friend" said Birch. "I must go now."

"Where will you go to?"

"I must join my father. There is no longer a place for men of magic here. You must be prepared to solve your own problems as and when they materialise. Look after Cat for me, for she will be a friend to you just as she has been a companion to me". Master Birch of the Timber Wood smiled, slowly faded, and then disappeared altogether.

"Let's go home" Said Aluen. Cat looked back for an instant to where Master Birch had stood, and then followed Aluen on his journey home.

★ ★ ★

In a place far removed from the daily problems of humankind, Master Elio welcomed Birch as he arrived.

"Can they survive by themselves, Master Elio?" asked Birch.

"It is time they learned. By the way, are you hungry?"

EPILOGUE

Master Elio had promised to give a parting present to the young lords, Master Errol, Master Terance and Lord Tamur before he left. He was true to his word. Each lord received a black-bladed sword which, at first glance appeared to be alive. But that couldn't be... or could it?

ND - #0476 - 270225 - C0 - 203/127/20 - PB - 9781861510945 - Matt Lamination